Jonathan Swift's

Gulliver's Travels

for Kids

Jonathan Swift's

Gulliver's Travels

for Kids

by Luke Hayes

J. Porter Publishing

J.Porter Publishing
250 Williams Road
Milan, New York 12571 USA

Classics for Kids: Gulliver's Travels for Kids by Luke Hayes

ISBN: 978-0-9831484-0-1

Printed in the United States of America on acid-free paper

For information: LukeHayesAuthor@gmail.com

Visit: http//:Gulliverstravelsforkids.com

Design: Joy Taylor   www.JoyTaylorDesign.com

Jonathan Swift's

Gulliver's Travels

for Kids

Part One

A Voyage to Lilliput

1

I can't think of anything more fun than going places. Can you?

Put me on the deck of a ship headed for adventure on the high seas, and I'm in heaven. When I was a boy in London, I used to spend every spare minute looking at maps and reading about faraway places. I could see myself exploring distant lands and meeting strange people.

Now I, Lemuel Gulliver, was on the greatest journey of my life. I had sailed to the other side of the world. So why was I so miserable? Why did I want more than anything to be back home?

I'll tell you why. Our ship, the *Antelope,* was being lashed by the worst storm I had ever seen. The white-capped waves lifted us up and crashed us down. I thought the wind would blow the hair off my head. We were lost somewhere off the coast of Australia. The waters were far too shallow for a great sailing ship. When the waves dropped, we could see sharp rocks sticking out. We were doomed!

Our captain, William Prichard, was a fine sailor. But even he was scared.

"The wind is blowing us right toward those rocks!" he shouted. "Helmsman, hard to starboard!"

"Look out!" cried a sailor. "We're going to crash!"

In the next few seconds, my whole life flashed in front of my eyes.

This is what I remembered: I had grown up in London in the late 1600's. That seems like a long time ago now, I know. My father tried to send me to school at Cambridge, but we were too poor and I had to drop out. Instead, when I was seventeen, I became an apprentice to Doctor James Bates. I was going to learn how to be a surgeon.

I studied in Holland, and Dr. Bates taught me how to treat wounds and mend broken legs and all that. But what I really wanted to do was to travel. I studied medicine, but I also studied navigation. I kept look-ing at maps and dreaming. I read tales of travelers and envied them.

After I finished my studies with Doctor Bates, I began to have patients of my own to take care of. My wife Mary and I settled in London and had two children, Johnny and Betty. But Mary knew I had always wanted to travel, so she urged me to go to sea.

"I'll do it!" I told her.

I signed up as ship's doctor and took several journeys to the Middle East and the West Indies. It wasn't a bad job, I'll tell you that. I always took a lot of books with me and I had many hours to relax and read. I learned to speak foreign languages. I learned about sailing. I found out about the many strange ways of people in other countries.

These trips left me wanting more. I made a little money, but I didn't get to see any of the really wild parts of the earth. The ships stuck to the usual trading routes while I patched up sailors who fell from the masts or the ones who took sick. I was eager for adventure.

That was why I agreed to go with Captain Prichard to the farthest ends of the earth. We set out on a nice spring morning, May 4, 1699, from the English port of Bristol. It wasn't until November that we reached the distant seas, where we planned to trade for spices. Down there, the seasons are reversed and it was the beginning of summer.

But the journey was difficult. By the fifth of November we were already in bad shape. We were running out of food and twelve sailors had died of hard labor. The rest of us were weak. We were sailing through strange, unknown waters. The storm drove us forward. The sea turned green. The sky dropped toward us like the palm of a hand. Mist thickened the air.

The gale was blowing hard. The *Antelope* leaned over so far you couldn't walk her deck without hanging on. Waves crashed. Our sails flapped so hard that several of them tore. And now we were rushing toward the rocks.

"Look out!"

Too late. The ship crashed with an awful crunching sound. Water rushed into the gash and we began to sink. I helped five other sailors to put down the lifeboat. We climbed in. We rowed hard to get clear of the rocks.

We rowed and rowed—a good nine miles, I would guess. We were weak when we started, now we were exhausted. All we could do then was to let the boat drift.

We thought the storm was dying down, but soon the wind began to blow hard again. The waves mounted high. They snarled at us, frothing like mad dogs.

"Oh, no!" one of my companions yelled. A wave came crashing down on us. It smashed into the boat like a watery fist. In an instant, we were all in the water. We swam for dear life.

I don't know what happened to the others. I guess they were drowned. I swam as best I could, pushed along by the tide and wind. I thought it was only a matter of time before I went under myself.

I swam and swam. Many times I let down my legs and tried to touch bottom, but the water was too deep. I've never felt so lost in my life.

Finally, I had to give up. I was too tired to swim any longer. As I began to sink into the ocean, I suddenly felt the bottom! The water now was barely over my head. With a few more strokes, I reached a place where I could stand.

Luckily, the storm was passing. The sea grew calmer.

I walked along through the water. It grew shallower little by little, but I had to walk almost a mile before I reached the shore of a low-lying island.

I crawled onto the beach, thanking my lucky stars that I was alive. It was about eight at night and just getting dark. I walked about half a mile but saw no houses nor any sign that there were people on the island.

I was so tired I could not bear to take another step. The night was very warm. I lay down on some short, soft grass and fell asleep. I don't think I've ever slept so soundly in my life.

I must have been asleep for at least nine hours. When I awoke, the sun was just coming up. I felt better.

The only thing was, my nose itched like anything. I went to scratch it and found I could not move my arm. What in the world?

I wanted to get up, but I couldn't budge. My arms and legs were pinned to the ground!

I tried to move my head to see what was going on. I couldn't. My hair, which was long and thick, was fastened tightly to the ground. I could feel cords stretched across my chest and legs holding me fast.

You can imagine how I felt. I struggled, but I couldn't stir an inch. I couldn't even look around. The sun was climbing the sky and growing hot. I had to squint to keep it out of my eyes.

I could hear strange noises around me. Was it an animal? I heard squeaks and squeals. I couldn't see what it was because I couldn't lift my head.

I lay there looking up at the blue sky and wondering what was going on. Next, I felt something alive crawling on my leg. Oh, no! It crept, little by little up my body until it was near my throat.

I looked downward with my eyes and saw, peeking over my chin, a little man! He was barely six inches tall. He had a bow in his hand, with a little arrow ready to shoot. He was gazing at me, his eyes wide with curiosity.

Now I felt others, maybe forty in all, following him. I was so surprised that I gave out a terrible roar. The little men panicked. They leaped off me in fright. Several of them were injured jumping from my sides.

But seeing that I was pinned securely to the ground, one of them dared to return. When he came close to my face he threw up his hands in wonder and shouted, *Hekinah degul!* The others repeated his words several times. I had no idea what they meant.

I was very fearful myself and I began to struggle to get free. Finally, I was able to break the strings and pull up the pegs that held my left arm. I wrenched my head to the right. Boy, did that hurt! It pulled my hair something awful. But it also let me move my head a few inches so I could look around.

I tried to grab hold of some of the little men, but they scurried out of reach. I heard one of them cry out, *Togo phonac!*

At the same instant, I felt more than a hundred arrows prick my hand. They stung like needles. Others fell onto my face, which I tried to cover with my left arm.

Now I was really alarmed. I groaned with pain and struggled to get free. They shot more arrows. Some of them tried to stick me in the sides with spears, but I was wearing a thick leather vest that they couldn't get through.

I decided to lie still. When night came, I could use my left hand to pull up the rest of the pegs and free myself. If it came to a fight, I was so much bigger than these people, I could easily stand up against an entire army of them.

When they saw I was quiet, they stopped shooting arrows. But they didn't go away. By the noise, I could tell that lots more of them were gathering.

After a while I heard hammering. I turned my head as far as I could. I saw they had erected a small platform a few yards away from my right ear. Four of the little people climbed a ladder to stand on the small stage.

One of the men was taller than the rest by about an inch. He was dressed in rich clothes and had an assistant who attended him. The other two, dressed like noblemen, stood on either side.

Langro dehul san! the man said. This was the beginning of a long speech. I couldn't understand a word, of course. Sometimes he seemed to be threatening me. Other times, I thought he was speaking kindly. I later learned that he was telling me that I had come to the kingdom of Lilliput. I had never heard of such a place.

When he finished, I answered him, though I was sure he couldn't understand me, either.

"I will not resist," I assured him. I raised my hand to the sun as if swearing on it.

My first concern, since it had been so long since I'd eaten, was to try to get some food. I opened my mouth and pointed toward it with my finger.

The nobleman who had spoken, a *Hurgo* they called him, understood. He climbed down and ordered that ladders should be put up my sides. Hundreds of little people climbed up and brought me baskets full of meat. It seems the King had ordered this food to be ready when he first heard of me.

I ate the chunks of meat, which tasted like mutton. The loaves of bread were no bigger than musket balls. Three of them hardly made a mouthful. As they fed me, they kept crying out with wonder that I could eat so much.

I made a sign that I was thirsty. They rolled a whole barrel of wine near my hand and removed the lid. It only held a half pint, so I drank it right down. I found it much more delicious than our best wine back home.

They rolled up another barrel and I drank that. I could have taken more, but that was all they had.

All of this seemed to amuse them greatly. They danced on my chest and shouted, *Hekinah degul!* a few more times.

I have to admit that at times I felt like grabbing a bunch of them and smashing them against the ground. But I remembered how those arrows felt. And I now felt grateful that they had been kind enough to give me food and wine.

In fact, I was thinking these little people were very brave to even come near me. I must have appeared huge to them, though I'm no taller than the average man.

Next, another nobleman climbed onto my leg and walked up toward my face with about a dozen others. He had a message from the Emperor. At least, I guessed as much because he showed me a paper with an official seal. He spoke for ten minutes, pointing frequently toward the distance.

I didn't understand him and he didn't understand my answer. I made a motion with my hand, trying to get across the idea that what I wanted next was my freedom

I guess he understood the gesture because he shook his head. He signaled to me that I must be taken somewhere as a prisoner. But he seemed to be trying to show me I would be given enough to eat and drink.

I sure didn't want to remain a prisoner. But I could still feel the sting of their arrows in my hands and face. So I tried to show that I would go along with whatever they planned for me.

The Hurgo seemed happy at this.

Now, I had been lying for many hours without a chance to pee.

You can probably guess what I needed to do next. I was able to make the nobleman understand before he and his men climbed down. He ordered that the cords holding my left side should be loosened.

I was able to roll over onto my right side. The people there immediately saw what I was about to do and moved way back. They were amazed by the great stream that came pouring from me. To them, it was like a mighty river.

Well, that was a relief! When I rolled back, the little people applied an ointment to my hands and face that took away the pain of their arrows. I felt more comfortable, having eaten and drunk my fill. Soon I fell off to sleep.

Later I learned that the Emperor had ordered his men to mix a sleeping potion with the wine they gave me. He had also commanded them to bring me to the Capital city of his Empire.

All this made me think his Majesty was really quite wise. If those little men had tried to kill me with their tiny arrows and spears while I first slept, I would have woken up. In my rage, I would have broken any strings that held me down. After that, I could have killed them. It was smarter for them to treat me kindly.

Now, those people did not have all the modern inventions that we have, but they were very smart and ingenious. They built great ships in the forest where the wood was. By great I mean all of nine feet long. Then they moved them to the sea on large wagons that they constructed.

When they saw how big I was, they set five hundred carpenters to work making one of those wagons. It had a wooden frame raised three inches off the ground. The bed of the wagon was seven feet long and four feet wide. It moved on twenty-two small wheels.

When the wagon arrived, they set up eighty poles, each one foot high, around my body. They placed strips of cloth under my neck, my body, my arms and legs. To these they attached cords not much thicker than thread and ran them through pulleys attached to the poles. Nine hundred of their strongest men hauled on these lines, raising me a few inches off the ground.

They did all of this while I lay in a deep sleep and only told me about it later. The sleeping potion kept me from waking while they moved me.

They pushed the wagon under me and lowered me onto it. Next they hitched to the wagon fifteen hundred of their strongest horses, each of them about four-and-a-half inches high. They began to pull me toward the capital, which was about half a mile away.

I would have slept through the whole trip except for one thing. When the Emperor's servants stopped to adjust the wagon, two young men climbed up near my face to have a closer look. One of them stuck his staff up my nose. It was about the size of a piece of straw and made me sneeze like the dickens. Were they ever scared!

I awoke and saw what they were doing. It felt odd to lie there and be pulled along by little horses.

On we went. When we stopped to rest at night, five hundred guards were posted at my side with torches and bows and arrows. The next day we approached the city gates about noon. We stopped when we were two hundred yards away. The Emperor and his great officers came out to meet us.

The Emperor climbed onto a tower across the road to view me. All of his noble lords were with him. At least a hundred thousand of the city's residents came out as well. Everybody wanted to look at me. They set up ladders and at least ten thousand of them climbed up on top of me. I was glad when the Emperor passed a law against it.

There was a large stone building nearby, a temple that they no longer used. It was empty and not in very good shape. They decided that I should live there because it was one of their biggest buildings. The door was about four feet high and two feet wide, so I could crawl inside to sleep.

To keep me captive, they linked together ninety-nine chains, each about the size a lady's watch would hang on in our country. They locked them to my left ankle with thirty-six strong padlocks. Once they knew the chains would hold, they cut all the strings that held me down.

I rose. You can't imagine the shout that went up when those people saw me stand. Some cheered, some screamed in terror as I towered over them.

Even more noise broke out when I walked. The chains allowed me to move about six feet in any direction. I strolled up and down. It felt good to finally take a few steps and stretch my arms and legs.

At the end of the day, the people went home and I crawled into my house to lie down. There I was, a prisoner in the strangest land anyone had ever heard of.

I didn't see how I would ever get free or return home. I might never see Mary or Johnny or little Betty again. I began to think that traveling around the world wasn't such a wonderful thing after all.

2

When I awoke the next morning, I felt better. This was a beautiful country, like a big garden with lovely fields and meadows. The highest trees in the woods were about seven feet tall. I could see the capital city in the distance. It was as pretty as a picture in a book.

One thing troubled me. I had not had a chance to answer the call of nature for more than two days. I felt a griping in my stomach and a terrible need to go. But many curious townspeople had already come out from the city to see me, so I was ashamed to do it in public.

I would not write about this, dear reader, but I have promised to tell you every detail. And I know you must be curious about it.

In my urgent need, I crept into my house and did it there. I didn't like doing so, but I had no choice. After my hosts cleaned up that mess, I came on a better solution.

Early in the morning, before anyone was around, I would go as far as my chain would let me. There I would squat down and relieve myself. Two servants came soon after and shoveled the smelly waste into wheelbarrows and carried it off.

Now the Emperor came out again to have a closer look at me. He rode up on his horse. But the animal was so frightened at the size of me that he reared up and almost threw His Majesty to the ground. The Emperor dismounted and walked this way and that, staring at me, but always keeping a safe distance away.

The Empress and the young princes and princesses came as well. They were dressed in magnificent silk clothing and seated in closed chairs with handles carried by eight men. They all watched me from a good distance. I must have looked as big as a mountain to them.

While the Emperor was looking at me, I was studying him. I lay on my side to get a better look. He was a handsome man, a bit taller than most of his subjects. He dressed in plain but fine garments. Their style was part European and part oriental.

He pulled out his sword, a little dagger about three inches long. Its handle was covered in tiny diamonds. He had a good deal to say to me.

When he finished, I answered, "I cannot understand you, your Majesty. But I want you to know I do not mean you or your subjects any harm. I am but a poor shipwrecked sailor. I thank you humbly for feeding me and giving me a place to stay."

I said this in all the languages I knew—German, Dutch, Latin, French, Spanish, Italian. Neither the Emperor nor any of his ministers understood me any better than I understood them.

Before he went back home, the Emperor ordered guards to stay around me. It wasn't to keep a watch on me, but to protect me. Plenty of his subjects wanted to get near me and annoy me. Some of them even shot arrows at me as I sat on the ground outside my house. I don't know why. One of the arrows stung my cheek, just missing my left eye.

"Arrest those men!" the colonel of the guards commanded. At least, I assume that's what he meant.

His men ran over and grabbed the young men who had been firing the arrows.

"What shall we do with them, Colonel?"

"Tie them up and hand them over to the monster," I think he said. "That will be a fit punishment."

The soldiers shoved them toward me. I took them up in my hand and put five of them in my coat pocket. The sixth I held in front of me.

"Oh, no!" the little man cried. "Please don't hurt me."

I made a nasty face at him. I pretended I was going to eat him up. You should have heard him squeal. When I took out my penknife, he thought I was going to slice him to pieces. Instead, I cut the strings they had used to tie him. I set him gently on the ground. He ran away as fast as his legs would carry him.

I did the same to the others, giving each a good scare before letting him go. The people who saw this were happy that I was so forgiving. Word spread through the capital that I was a good person and not someone to be afraid of.

The floor of my house was stone, not so comfortable for sleeping. The Emperor was kind enough to order a bed made for me. His men brought six hundred mattresses. They laid a hundred and fifty of them out on the floor and sewed them together. On top of them, they put another hundred and fifty, sewing them together as well. Then another hundred and fifty and another.

Even with the mattresses stacked four thick like that, they were so thin that they didn't provide much comfort. But in my travels I was used to difficult conditions, so it didn't bother me.

So many people were coming to see me from around the Empire that not much work was getting done on the whole island. The Emperor had to order anyone who had already seen me to go home and not return without permission. Some of his ministers began to charge people money to look at me.

All this time, the noblemen of the Empire were discussing what to do with me.

"He'll get loose!" some warned.

"He eats too much," said others. "If we keep feeding him, there won't be enough food for us."

"Let's starve him to death."

"No, let's shoot him in the face and hands with poison arrows."

"But if we do that, his body will stink and make everybody sick."

About that time, someone came in to make a report about me. He told them about the rascals who had shot arrows at me.

"The monster treated them with mercy, your Majesty. We think he is almost as human as we are, though of monstrous size."

"I decree that this monster should be fed every day," the Emperor said. "We have enough food in our kingdom. Each village shall send a portion of bread, meat and wine each day. The royal treasury will pay for it."

So every morning six beeves, forty sheep, and plenty of bread and wine arrived at my house, all paid for by the Emperor.

That wasn't all. Six hundred people were chosen to be my servants.

They all lived in tents outside my house. Three hundred tailors sewed me a new suit of clothes. Six of the smartest college professors taught me to speak their language.

After about three weeks of instruction, I could understand it well enough. The Emperor himself came to talk with me and help me learn. As soon as I knew a few words, I knelt before him.

"I am very grateful to your Majesty for all your kindness," I said in his own language.

"You have remained peaceful," he replied, "so we have treated you as a guest. Is there anything else you need?"

"Please, your Majesty," I said. "I ask only one thing. Let me have my freedom."

"Now, that's impossible. I cannot put the lives of my subjects at risk. Once we know you better, perhaps we can give you more liberty."

Lumos Kelmin pesso desmar lon emposo, he said. He meant that I had to swear to be peaceful for as long as I was in his Empire.

He also told me that his men must search me. They wanted to know if I was carrying any dangerous weapons.

"If you will let them," he said in his language, "two of my officers will examine you. Anything they take will be returned to you when you leave my kingdom."

I agreed. I picked up the officers and placed them first in my coat pocket. Then I moved them to every other pocket, except a secret pocket that I didn't want them to search.

They wrote down everything that they found and then made a report to the Emperor.

"We have searched *Quinbus Flestrin*," they began. That's what they called me. The words meant "Man-Mountain."

"In the right pocket we found a great piece of coarse cloth. It could serve as a carpet for the largest room in your Majesty's palace."

By this, they meant my handkerchief.

"In the left pocket we found a huge silver chest. The lid was so heavy, we couldn't lift it. When Quinbus opened it, we stepped inside and found ourselves up to our knees in brown dust. Some of it flew into the air and made us sneeze awfully."

They were describing my snuff box.

"In another pocket we found a bundle of white sheets as big as three men and held with strong rope. These sheets were marked with black figures. We think it is writing. Each letter was as larger than the palm of our hands."

This was my notebook.

"We found a strange object with twenty long poles that looked like a picket fence. We think the Man-Mountain uses this to comb his hair. We're not sure."

They were correct.

"In another pocket we found a piece of iron pipe about as long as a man. It's attached to a large mass of timber. On the side are iron gadgets of strange design. We don't know what it is, but he has another in his opposite pocket."

They meant my pistols. In Lilliput, guns were not known.

"In the pockets of his trousers we found flat metal disks so big and heavy one man couldn't lift one."

They were talking about some coins I had.

"The narrow pockets of his vest we could not enter. Quinbus Flestrin drew from one of them a marvelous engine on a huge silver chain. It was partly made of silver and partly of a metal that can be seen through. We saw strange figures drawn in a circle. When we put our ears to this engine, we could hear a loud sound like a watermill makes."

This, of course, was my watch. Those people had no watches, and no glass, either.

"There may be an animal inside," they went on. "Or it may be the god he worships. He told us, if we understand him, that he seldom does anything without looking first at this machine. He said it told him when to do things."

"Very interesting," the King remarked.

"In his other vest pocket he carried an enormous purse in which are several pieces of metal. If they are real gold, as they appear to be, they are very valuable indeed."

I did carry a few pieces of gold in my purse.

"Around his waist, the Man-Mountain wears a strip of hide that must come from an enormous animal. Attached on one side is a sword as long as five men. On the other is a box with two containers that could hold three men each. In one container we found balls of heavy metal about the size of a man's head. In the other were heaped coarse black grains of a substance we had never seen before."

They were here referring to my ammunition case, in which I carried gunpowder and balls for my pistols.

"Quinbus Flestrin," the Emperor said, "must now give up everything and anything that could be used to harm our subjects."

He had three thousand of his best troops standing by with bows and arrows in case I used any of the weapons.

First I took off my sword and waved it in my hand. It was still bright, though the sea water had rusted it a bit. The reflection of the sun on the blade made the Emperor's men cry out in fright. They knew I could do great damage to them with it.

"Toss that awful blade onto the ground out of your reach," the Emperor ordered. I did what I was told.

"What about those pieces of iron pipe in your pocket? Could they be dangerous?"

"I will show you, if you'll let me."

I took out one of my pocket pistols and loaded it with gunpowder only, no bullet. Fortunately my ammunition case was waterproof and the powder still good.

"Don't be afraid, your Majesty," I said. "This is going to be very loud."

I pointed the pistol into the air and fired. Oh, were they surprised! For them, it was like a cannon going off. They had never heard anything like it. Hundreds of men fell to the ground as if they had been shot. Even the Emperor was rattled.

I handed over my pistols and ammunition. I said, "I must warn his Majesty to be sure the black powder is kept safe from fire. Even the smallest spark will blow your palace to bits."

They took my watch, which two tall servants carried between them on a pole. The Emperor was amazed at the noise it made. He studied the movement of the minute hand.

I handed over my comb, my purse, my handkerchief and notebook. The one secret pocket that they did not search contained my eyeglasses. I have to admit that my eyesight is a bit weak and I wanted them close at hand. I also had a small telescope and several other personal objects that I was afraid might be spoiled if taken away.

"Take the giant's blade to be locked in the palace," the Emperor ordered. "And those magical iron pipes he calls his pistols. Return everything else to him."

But he didn't give me back my most important possession of all: my freedom.

3

I made a plan to win my liberty. I would act as pleasant and peaceful as possible. As the people got used to me, they would no longer be afraid. I was making good progress learning their language, so I could talk and joke with them.

Sometimes I would let five or six of them dance on my hand. When I stretched out on the ground, boys and girls would come and play hide-and-seek in my hair. I could hear them giggling and giving light tugs on my locks.

After a while, the Emperor invited me to watch one of their most popular shows. It seems these folks have a strange custom. When a job comes open in the Emperor's court, the top candidates for the position have to show their ability to dance on a tightrope.

The narrow rope is about two feet long and is strung twelve inches off the ground. That doesn't sound high, but for them it's the same as twelve feet would be for us.

The person who is able to perform the best is the one who gets the job. Don't ask me why they do it this way. We, of course, have a much smarter method.

All the high government officials have to practice their skills at tightrope dancing. One of the best was Flimnap, the Treasurer of the Empire. I have seen him turn two somersaults on a small platform set on the rope. My friend Reldresal, Secretary of Private Affairs, is another brilliant performer.

These acts are very dangerous. The ministers try so hard to outdo each other that they often fall, and a fall of twelve inches can kill these people. I have personally seen several candidates break their arms and legs. Before my arrival, Flimnap himself took a tumble. He would have broken his neck if he had not landed on one of the King's cushions.

The candidates for office go through another test, too. In this one, the Emperor holds one end of a stick and the first minister holds another. Candidates for office must either leap over the stick or creep under it. The ones who do best are given red, blue or green ribbons.

These little people love shows of all kinds. As the Emperor grew to trust me more and more, he allowed me to join in. For example, the army's best mounted troops would charge at my hand on their horses and leap over it. One of their strongest horses was actually able to jump over my foot. They all cheered to see it.

Another time I made a stage by placing my handkerchief over a frame I had built of sticks, about two and a half feet square. I pulled the cloth so tight that it could hold up a whole troop of men on horseback. I set up parallel sticks around the edges to keep them from falling off. They fought mock battles, shooting blunt arrows and waving their swords.

The Emperor loved this show. Even the Empress allowed me to hold her up in her closed chair so she could watch.

It all went well until one of the fiery horses pawed with his hoof and tore a hole in my handkerchief. He fell and threw his rider. I repaired my handkerchief, but I didn't trust it any longer to hold up horsemen.

Once, while I was entertaining the Emperor and some members of his court, two horsemen rode up.

"Some of your subjects of the other side of the kingdom have discovered a strange object, your Majesty," they reported. "It's black and as big as your Majesty's bedroom. In the middle it rises up as high as a man."

"At first we thought it might be alive," the other man said. "We figured it was another strange creature like the Man-Mountain. But it never moved. So we climbed up on each other's shoulders and were able to get to the top. We stomped around and found it was hollow."

"Maybe it belongs to the Man-Mountain," the first said.

"If your Majesty please, we can bring it to the capital. It will take five horses to pull it."

"I know exactly what it is, your Majesty." I explained that my hat, tied with a string, had stayed on after the ship sank and all the time I was swimming. But when I came on land, the string must have broken. It fell off and I had had nothing since to protect my head from the sun.

"I would be very grateful if you would have it brought to me."

The men arrived with it the next day. They had bored two holes in the brim to fasten it to the harness. Then the horses had dragged it half a mile. Still, it was good enough to wear and I was glad to have it back.

The next day, the Emperor got an idea for another show. He wanted me to stand like a giant statue with my legs apart. Then he got his top general to march his army between my legs. Three thousand men and a thousand horses passed through in a long parade. They had flags flying and drums beating.

I wonder why some of the young officers are laughing? I said to myself. And they keep elbowing each other and pointing. It doesn't seem very good form during a parade.

Then I realized that as they passed under me, they were looking up. I had not yet received the new suit of clothes the tailors were sewing for me. My old pants were in awful shape, full of holes. It must have made an amusing sight for the soldiers, but I was ashamed.

All this time, remember, I remained chained. I kept begging the Emperor to give me my freedom. But there was a problem, a big problem. One of the ministers at the Emperor's court had become my mortal enemy. I don't know why. He just didn't like me.

This man's name was Skyresh Bolgolam. He held the position of *Galbet* which is what they called the Admiral of their navy. He was a powerful man, but very sour and disagreeable.

"We all think Quinbus Flestrin should be allowed his freedom," one of the ministers said during a meeting. "He has remained peaceful and acted very courteous toward his Majesty's subjects."

"No, he must remain a prisoner," Bolgolam replied. "Who knows the damage he could do if he got free."

Finally, they convinced him to let me go, but only if I swore to certain conditions.

One of the ministers was sent to my house with an official document. After he cleared his throat a few times, he read: "In the name of Golbasto Mully Ully Gue, the mighty emperor of Lilliput, Terror of the Universe."

That was the Emperor's name. It sounded silly to me, but he and his subjects laughed when I told them my name was Lemuel Gulliver. It's a perfectly ordinary name, but they thought it absurd.

"The Mighty Emperor, who rules over the whole world and whose head strikes the sun, demands that Quinbus Flestrin, who has come to our realm, should swear by solemn oath to do the following. Ahem."

He cleared his throat once more.

"He shall not leave our kingdom without permission. He shall not come into the capital city without our order, and shall give the people there two hours notice so that they can keep indoors. He shall walk only on the roads and not on the gardens or fields of grain. He shall be careful not to trample on our citizens."

These were all reasonable conditions, I thought.

"Furthermore, if an urgent message needs to be delivered, the Man-Mountain shall carry the messenger in his pocket and bring him back in order to help him speed up his duty. He shall aid us in fighting our enemies if they try to invade. He shall help our workmen move great stones. And he shall walk around our realm to give us the exact distance that our borders cover."

These conditions I didn't like so well. I was a doctor, not a common laborer. Not a messenger boy.

"If Quinbus Flestrin swears to abide by all these conditions, he shall have a daily allowance of meat and drink, enough to support 1,728 of our subjects."

They later explained to me how they calculated this number. They were less than six inches high, I was not quite six feet. That meant I was twelve times as tall. But as I had learned in geometry class, to find the volume you must cube the number. That means multiplying it by itself twice. Twelve times twelve is 144. Twelve times 144 is 1,728. This made me realize that these people were quite as smart as any European, though we always think we're the smartest in the world.

"On my oath," I said, "I agree to these conditions."

That, the man said, was not good enough. In Lilliput, a person swears by taking his right foot in his left hand and placing the middle finger of his right hand on the top of his head. He also sticks his right thumb in his ear. It seemed weird, but I did it.

Sure enough, as soon as I swore, they unlocked the chain. I was free at last. Now I was anxious to explore this strange, strange land.

The first thing I wanted to do was to see Mildendo, their capital city. The Emperor said I could if I did not hurt any of the people there, or damage their houses. He let everybody know I was coming.

The wall around the city stood two and a half feet high and was eleven inches thick. Every ten feet was a strong tower. I took off my coat so that it wouldn't brush against any buildings. I stepped over the gate and moved sideways along the main street.

Almost everybody was indoors, but I stepped carefully in case someone might be still in the street. The windows of the buildings and all the roofs were crowded with people looking out to see me. I was amazed how many people lived there. I estimated the population was five hundred thousand souls.

I couldn't go down the side streets or alleys because they were too narrow. The two main streets were five feet wide. Their houses, which are between three and five stories high, came up to my waist.

In the center of the city was the Emperor's palace. It was enclosed by another wall two feet high. There was a courtyard inside about twenty feet wide.

"I would like to show you the inner court of the palace, where the Empress and I live," he told me. "But I don't see how you could climb in without knocking into the buildings."

"I will find a way, your Majesty."

My solution was to make two stools from stout trees. They were each three feet high. I placed one on each side of the buildings and stepped over.

In the inner court, I lay down on my side. That way I could look through the windows of the palace. I saw very splendid rooms. I also saw the Empress and the young princes. Her Majesty even put her hand out the window so that I could kiss it.

About two weeks after I was given my freedom, I was visited by Reldresal, the First Secretary of Private Affairs. He had always been my friend and had spoken well of me in the Emperor's court.

"I want to have a private talk with you," he said.

"I'll lie down so that you can speak into my ear."

"You don't need to do that. Just hold me in your hand while we talk."

I lifted him up.

"The reason you were not released earlier," he said, "is in part because the Kingdom of Lilliput is facing some very serious dangers. First, certain people here are staging a revolt."

"But why? This seems like such a peaceful place."

"There are two political parties in the kingdom. One is the High-heelers, the other the Low-heelers. The Emperor believes in low heels on his shoes. But many of his subjects favor high heels. Even the prince, who is heir to the throne, now goes around with one high and one low heel. He tries to appeal to both factions, even though it makes him walk with a limp. The High-heelers are always complaining and talking against his Majesty."

"That seems like a silly issue," I said.

"I can assure you, it's not. The other problem is that Lilliput is facing an invasion from its enemies on the island of Blefuscu. Blefuscu is the only other kingdom on earth and is almost as powerful as we are."

I had told him before that there were many other kingdoms in the world. But he said their philosophers couldn't believe that. In all their history, they had never heard of the strange places I spoke of. Their theory was that I had dropped down from the moon or the stars.

"Anyway, Lilliput and Blefuscu have been enemies for many years," he explained. "It began when the Emperor's grandfather decreed that anyone eating an egg in the kingdom should break it at the wide end, not the short end."

"What difference does it make?" I asked.

"All the difference in the world. The two ends are opposite, aren't they? The people in Blefuscu said it was wrong to break eggs at the wide end. It went against the teaching of their prophet *Lustrog* as written in the *Brundecral*, which is what you would call their Bible."

Eleven thousand Lilliputians had been executed, he said, because they believed in breaking their eggs at the wide end.

"Others fled to Blefuscu and encouraged the Emperor of that land to wage war on us. The war has been raging for years, with many ships sunk."

"I still don't see how eating eggs can be so important."

"It just is," he said. "Now the Emperor of Blefuscu is preparing a fleet to invade us. His Majesty hopes and prays that you will come to our aid. You are our only hope."

"I can't get involved in party politics," I told him. "But I will help to defend Lilliput against her enemies. Tell the Emperor that I await his orders."

He thanked me and hurried back to the palace. I sat there wondering what I was getting into.

5

The Island of Blefuscu was located northeast of Lilliput, about half a mile away. I kept away from that side of the island so that I would not be seen by anyone on enemy ships. The people of Blefuscu knew nothing about me. During the war there was no trade between the two islands.

But spies had told the admirals of Lilliput that the Blefuscu fleet was preparing to cross to Lilliput and invade.

"How deep is the water out there?" I asked them.

"Seventy *glumgluffs*," they told me. I knew that was only about six feet in our measures.

I went over to that side of the island and lay down behind a hill. I got out the telescope I had hidden in my secret pocket. Through it, I could see fifty warships and many other ships for carrying soldiers.

Back at my house, I ordered them to bring me as much rope as possible. Because their thickest rope was only as thick as a cord, I twisted three strands of it together. I made fifty hooks out of bars of iron they brought me.

I went back to the far coast and took off my coat and my shoes and socks. I waded in, taking my ropes and hooks. I had to swim for a way in the middle, but in half an hour I was close to the shore of Blefuscu.

The sailors in the warships were so scared to see me that they jumped into the water and swam ashore. I took my hooks and fastened each one to the front of one of the ships. While I was doing this, they began to shoot arrows at me. They hit me in the face and hands. That hurt like anything. I almost gave up because of the pain.

I was most afraid that they might hit me in the eye and blind me. I thought of a solution. I took out my spectacles and put them on. Many of their arrows struck the glass of my spectacles, but did me no harm. I was in pain, but I kept at it.

I now had all the ships fastened to ropes. I tugged, but they would not move. They were held by their anchors. While I was cutting the anchor ropes, the men shot many more arrows into my hands and face. But I soon freed all the ships and was easily able to pull them away through the water.

When they saw me taking away their ships, the people of Blefuscu let out a scream. They knew they were lost.

As soon as I got out of danger, I stopped to pull the arrows from my hands and face. I rubbed the wounds with ointment that the Emperor had given me. I took off my spectacles and returned them to my pocket.

By that time the tide had gone down and I could wade all the way back to the main port of Lilliput. The Emperor and a huge crowd of people were there to meet me. At first, seeing the ships of Blefuscu coming, they were afraid. They couldn't see me pulling them because I was so low. But as the water grew shallower, they realized I had completely defeated the people of Blefuscu.

"Long live the Emperor of Lilliput!" I called out.

The people cheered.

"I hereby proclaim," the Emperor said, "that for his great service to the Kingdom of Lilliput, Quinbus Flestrin shall, from this day forward, be a *Nardac* of our realm."

Everyone cheered again. I was told that the title of Nardac is the highest honor they can give a person.

"Now," the Emperor went on, "I order that Quinbus Flestrin should destroy the Empire of Blefuscu completely. He shall help us make all of the people there eat their eggs from the wide end."

"I can't do that, your Majesty," I said. "I told you I would help protect your kingdom. But I will not force a free people to become your subjects."

The high officials of Lilliput discussed the matter and most agreed with me. Better to end the war and live in peace.

But I could tell that the Emperor did not like anyone to defy his wishes. Several of his ministers were already talking against me in the court. Now they began a serious plot.

About three weeks after I brought the ships across, some officials came from Blefuscu to ask for peace. They signed a treaty that finally ended the war.

These officials heard that I had refused to help the king of Lilliput to enslave their people. They came to me after signing the treaty.

"We want to thank you for your mercy, Mister Monster," they said.

The ministers of Blefuscu spoke through an interpreter. The two countries had their own languages, just like different countries in Europe. And just like in Europe, they each thought their language was the best and most beautiful. Someone had to translate their words into the language of Lilliput so that I could understand.

"The Emperor of Blefuscu would like to invite you to visit his Kingdom," they said.

I told them that I would pay them a visit before I returned to my own country. Later, I asked the Emperor of Lilliput for permission to visit Blefuscu.

"You can go, if you choose," he said.

He was very cold toward me. I didn't know why at the time. Later I learned that Flimnap and Bolgolam, my enemies in the court, had told the Emperor that I was disloyal. They said that my talks with the ministers of Blefuscu proved it.

Now, the Emperor of Lilliput had never asked me to do any of the low tasks that I had agreed to, like delivering messages or moving stones around. But soon afterward, I was able to do him a great favor.

This is what happened. I awoke about midnight to hear loud cries and hundreds of people around my door. I woke up in terror.

I kept hearing them say, *Burglum! Burglum!* I knew what this meant. Fire!

"Come to the Emperor's palace," they shouted to me. "It's burning!"

A careless maid had fallen asleep while reading a book. Her candle had started a fire in the palace.

I reached the palace. Fortunately, the bright moon let me see the many people who were running around, and I didn't step on any. I saw that they were fighting the fire with a bucket brigade. I tried to help, but the buckets were no bigger than a thimble. The flames were raging and the little splashes of water did no good.

I could see that the magnificent palace was sure to burn to the ground. But then I thought of something. I had drunk a good deal of their excellent wine before going to bed. They call it *glimigrim* and it really is delicious. So guess what? I needed to pee. Bad.

In the next instant, I was peeing on the fire. I had such a large quantity in me that I became a human fire extinguisher. In a few minutes I had drenched all the flames and the fire was out.

I returned to my house without staying to talk to the Emperor. I figured he would be glad that I saved his palace. But what would he think about the *way* that I saved it?

The reason I was worried was that in Lilliput there was a law that made it a high crime to urinate within the palace. I knew the penalty was death.

My worries increased when I heard that the Empress swore that she would never move back into the damaged rooms, even if they were repaired. She told everyone that she would get revenge on me for what I had done.

6

Now, you're probably wondering exactly what the Kingdom of Lilliput is like. I've been meaning to tell you.

As I said, the people are less than six inches tall. That means that the horses and cows are only four or five inches high. The sheep are an inch and a half. Their geese are about the size of a sparrow in our country. Their songbirds are so small you can hardly see them.

Fortunately for the people there, their eyesight lets them see very sharply, but not very far. Their vision is so fine that I have seen a cook plucking a bird that was smaller than a housefly. A girl was able to thread the tiniest of needles with a thread that to my eyes was invisible.

The tallest trees there are about seven feet high. I can just barely reach their highest branches. Apple trees are only about a foot high and the grass is so short that it's like moss.

After I learned their language, I found out that the Lilliputians are very well educated. They have many books, but their writing is strange. They don't write from left to right like we do in Europe. They don't write from right to left the way Arabs do. They don't write up to down like the Chinese or down to up like the Cascagians. No, they write from one corner of the paper to the other, like some school children in our country who can't write in a straight line.

When they bury their dead, they put them in the grave head first. They think the earth is flat. In eleven thousand moons, it will flip over. Their dead will then be standing upright. The smartest of them think this is ridiculous, but they still do it.

Their laws are very strict. They are also very hard on anyone who makes a false accusation. If you accuse someone and that person turns out to be innocent, you are put to death yourself. They punish fraud much more harshly than theft. If a man runs off with money that has been entrusted to him, he is guilty of a terrible crime.

Once I was discussing our own legal system with my friend Reldresal.

"Our system has severe penalties," he said, "but it also has great rewards."

"What do you mean?" I asked.

"We reward people when they don't do wrong, or course. Don't you do that in your country?"

"No, in England we punish people for crimes and that's all."

"I find that hard to believe. Don't you think justice would work better if there were both rewards and punishments?"

I asked him how the rewards work.

"If you can prove that you've obeyed all the laws for seventy-three moons, about six years in your terms, you are awarded money. You are also given the title *Snilpall* which means *Legal One*. That gives you privileges in our kingdom and makes others respect you."

"It sounds like a good idea," I admitted.

"Of course it is. Much better than your system, I'm sure."

"What do you consider the worst crime?" I asked him.

"Not saying thank you for a favor," he said. "That's obviously the worst."

"Why?"

"Because anyone who's not grateful to someone who helps him out must be an enemy to everyone. Think how he'd treat someone who didn't help him out. So we think it's a serious crime."

I was glad I had been so polite since I had been in Lilliput. I asked him how they bring up their children.

"We don't think they owe anything to their parents," he said. "Nothing at all. And the parents we think are the worst people to bring up a child."

"What do you do with your children?"

"When they are two years old, they go off to school. The professors there see to their education and care for them. The kids wear plain clothes and learn honor, justice, courage, patriotism and good manners. They work all day long except for a two-hour play period. They are never allowed to fool around, that would only teach them how to be bad. Their parents can see them twice a year, for one hour only."

"Can the parents bring them toys or presents?"

"Oh, no. That's not allowed. If the child is to follow a trade, he becomes an apprentice at age seven. He might learn to be a goldsmith or a wagon maker or a printer. The children of noblemen stay at school until they reach age fifteen."

He told me that they had strict laws that forbad the servants who took care to the children to tell them frightening or foolish stories.

"No stories?" I said. "But children love stories."

"No, hearing stories only makes them silly and gives them crazy ideas. No stories, that's the law. If servants are caught telling stories, they're whipped in public, then imprisoned and forced to leave the city."

I thought that was way too much punishment for such a small offense. But I didn't tell him so.

"Both boys and girls are educated in the same way," he said.

"That's not true in our country," I told him. "Girls often don't get a proper education at all."

"That hardly seems right," he declared.

All this was quite interesting to me, but I was not surprised. I had learned in my travels that different people have very different customs. You may think a way of doing things is logical and smart. But you can't always figure that the folks of a distant land will agree with you.

As for my own house, I was able to build a table and chair by cutting down some of their tallest trees. The Lilliputians were kind enough to hire two hundred seamstresses to sew my shirts and a tablecloth. They had to piece together sections of cloth, because theirs came only three inches wide. They laid my old shirt on the ground and used that as a pattern. When they were done, all my clothes looked like the patchwork quilts we have back home.

Every day, three hundred cooks prepared my meals. They lived and cooked in huts built around my house. When it was dinner time, I placed twenty waiters on the table. A hundred more brought dishes of food. The waiters on the table pulled up the meat and wine and other things using ropes.

A dish of meat made one mouthful. Their mutton was not as good as ours, a bit dry. But their beef was actually better and tasted very tender. A sirloin steak, if it was a big one, I could eat in three bites, bone and all. I could eat a whole goose or turkey in a mouthful. They were very delicious.

One day, the Emperor and his wife and the young princes came to have dinner with me. I set them on the table along with their guards. Flimnap, the Treasurer, also came. He didn't like me, I knew, and kept staring at me with a sour look. Oh, he was very polite. But I knew he spoke against me to his Majesty.

"The Man-Mountain eats far too much," he said. "The kingdom will have to borrow money just to feed him. Your Majesty should get rid of this monster as soon as possible."

One reason he hated me, I found out, was that he thought his wife had fallen in love with me and was coming to see me secretly. This was utter nonsense. A lie. She did come to my house, but always publicly, usually with her sister and daughter. Many others came to visit me as well. I would take their carriages up and place them on my table, sometimes three or four at a time.

I had many agreeable conversations this way. But nobody ever came in secret except Reldresal, who was sent by the Emperor himself, as I have said, to warn of the invasion.

The nerve of that Flipnap, I said to myself. Why, I'm a *Nardac* and he's only a *Clumglum*. That's a less noble title. What right does he have to complain about me?

But Flimnap continued to hate me. What's worse, his whispering made the Emperor himself begin to suspect me. That put me in a very dangerous situation. I'll tell you all about it in the next chapter.

7

As a poor man, I had never in my life had anything to do with the courts of kings or emperors. I didn't know what kind of meanness and plotting went on there.

One night, a nobleman of Lilliput came secretly to my house. Even now, I refuse to say his name so that he won't get in trouble. I could see that he was very worried.

"You know," he said to me, "that Skyresh Bolgolam, the High Admiral has been your mortal enemy every since you arrived, don't you?"

"I can't understand why he doesn't like me. I helped him have a great victory over Blefuscu."

"But don't you see? That made him look bad. He wasn't able to defeat our enemies, but you were. He's jealous of your strength and power. He hates you. So does Flimnap, the High Treasurer, who still suspects that you have been dillydallying with his wife. They have gotten others of the Emperor's top advisors to turn against you. They are accusing you of treason!"

"What? Why I've done nothing but help Lilliput since the day I arrived."

"I know that. So do many others. But the high Lords of the court are plotting against you."

"I can't believe it."

"I think they are treating you unfairly. That's why I've brought you this. It's the list of charges against you. Read it."

He handed me a piece of paper. It said that Quinbus Flestrin, the Man-Mountain (meaning me) was accused of high crimes. Here's what they were:

1. The law says whoever shall make water within the royal palace

shall be guilty of treason. Quinbus, pretending to put out a fire, did spray his urine on his Majesty's palace.

2. After Quinbus brought the ships of Blefuscu into our port, his Majesty ordered him to enslave the people of Blefuscu and to put to death all who ate their eggs from the wide end. He refused.

3. When the ambassadors came from Blefuscu to make peace, Quinbus met with them and gave them aid and comfort, even though they were his Majesty's enemies.

4. Quinbus is now preparing to travel to Blefuscu in order to conspire with the Emperor of that land against Lilliput.

"All these charges are untrue," I said. "I did put out the fire at the palace. If I hadn't, it would have burned down. I defended Lilliput against Blefuscu. I met with the ambassadors only to be friendly and help make peace. I'm not planning to conspire with anybody. I'm only going there for a visit."

"I know that, but the Treasurer and the Admiral have argued against you. They insisted that you be put to death. They planned to send twenty thousand soldiers to shoot arrows into your hands and face, then set your house on fire. They also wanted to get your servants to put poison on your clothes to make you tear your own flesh and die in pain."

When I heard this, I became very afraid. These people were small, but they had the power to kill me easily if they wanted. For one thing, they could simply put poison in the food they gave me.

"Fortunately," he said, "your friend Reldresal spoke up for you. He said that his Majesty should show mercy to you."

"Oh, I'm so thankful to have at least one friend at the court."

"Yes, he said that they should not kill you, but only put out your eyes."

"What? My eyes?"

"He said you would be just as useful to the kingdom if you were blind. But Bolgolam, the Admiral, would not agree. He lost his temper and said you must be killed. If you turned against us, you could destroy the whole Empire of Lilliput. You could take the fleet right back to Blefuscu if you wanted. He even accused you of secretly eating your eggs from the wide end."

"What did the others say?"

"Flimnap, the Treasurer, said that we could no longer afford to keep you. If you were blinded, you would eat just as much or more. You must be killed, he said."

"Did Reldresal speak up for me?"

"Yes, he said there was no need to put you to death. If, after blinding you, we simply cut back your food, you would grow very thin and then die of starvation. Your body would be so shrunken that it would be easy to cut off your flesh and take it away to bury. So there would be no disease in the kingdom as a result of your rotting."

"What did the Emperor say?"

"He said that he felt mercy toward you and would decree that Reldresal's suggestion be carried out. In three days, they will come and inform you that your eyes must be put out. His Majesty assumes you will gladly allow this to be done."

"How?"

"By lying on the ground and allowing archers to shoot arrows into your eyeballs. Afterward, without telling you, they will begin to starve you to death."

He told me he had to return to the city right away. He was taking a great chance by coming to tell me. I thanked him for letting me know about the plot against me. He may have saved my life.

Now, the Emperor thought that he was being generous in not putting me to death right away. I didn't see it that way. I had committed no crimes and had helped Lilliput in many ways.

At first, I thought I would take up big stones and smash the entire capital to pieces, killing all the little people who lived there. But I could not do that. I had sworn an oath to be peaceful. And the Emperor had done me many favors, feeding me and giving me a place to live.

Instead, I hit on another plan. I already had permission to travel to Blefuscu. Instead of waiting, I set out for that island right away.

First, I went to the port and took one of the largest of Lilliput's war ships. I took off my clothes and loaded them on board. I pulled the ship after me, wading and swimming across the long channel.

When I reached Blefuscu, the people there were happy to see me. Two guides showed me the way to the capital, which is also called Blefuscu. When I was two hundred yards away, I asked them to inform the

Emperor of Blefuscu that I had arrived. An hour later he came out. I lay on the ground to kiss his hand and that of the Empress.

"I have come to visit your Majesty and to be of service to you if I can." I did not mention that I had been disgraced in Lilliput.

"You are welcome here, Mr. Monster, and I hope you will enjoy my kingdom and be comfortable here."

Well, I tried as I could to make myself comfortable, but I had no house or bed or blankets. I could do nothing but lie on the ground outdoors to sleep.

While I was lying looking up at the stars, I began to wish I was back home. If only I could think of some way of getting there. By a lucky accident, that way soon appeared. I'll tell about it in the next chapter.

8

I had been in Blefuscu three days and was taking a walk around the island to see what the land was like. I came near the northeast coast. Looking out at the sea, I thought I saw something. It was about a mile away and floating low in the water. Could it be a boat? An actual, full-sized boat, not one of their little bitty ones?

I quickly pulled off my shoes and stocking. I waded a quarter mile into the water. The tide was bringing the object nearer. Yes, it was a boat. It probably had been knocked off a ship in a storm. I could see that it was too big for me to handle myself.

I was excited. It was the first object from my own world I had seen in a long time.

I rushed back to land and went to his Imperial Majesty, the King of Blefuscu. I told him I had discovered something that would amaze him.

"Please, lend me twenty of your tallest ships," I pleaded. "And three thousand sailors to sail them."

He agreed.

The fleet began to sail around the island. I hurried back over land. When I got there, I wove together lengths of their heaviest ropes. When the ships arrived, I waded and swam to the floating boat. I tied the rope onto the bow of the boat and the other end to one of their ships.

The boat was upside down and filled with water.

"It won't move," one of the sailors said. "It's too heavy."

The water was over my head. I had to try to swim and push the boat at the same time. The Blefuscu ship did its best to pull it.

Once the water was shallow enough for me to stand, I was able to push harder. I took the other ropes I had made and tied them to the boat. The sailors then fastened them to nine other ships.

The wind was with us. They towed and I pushed until the boat was forty yards from shore. As soon as the tide went out, it rested on the sand. With the help of two thousand men pulling, I was able to turn it onto its bottom. I was happy to see that it was hardly damaged.

I was so used to seeing everything in miniature, that this boat looked huge even to me. I began to bail it out and soon had it floating.

It took me ten days to carve paddles out of tall trees with my pocket knife. I then rowed the boat over to the royal port of Blefuscu. The people there were amazed to see what was to them an enormous ship bigger than three or four of theirs.

I met with the Emperor of Blefuscu. "Fortune had brought me this boat so that I might reach a place where I can return to my own land," I told him. "I beg your Majesty to help me get the materials I needed to equip the boat. And I ask your permission to depart."

"You have my permission," he said. "And we will help you all we can."

While I was working to make the boat seaworthy, the Emperor of Lilliput began to suspect that I had discovered the charges against me. He was right. He realized I was staying in Blefuscu to avoid the punishment of having my eyes put out.

An ambassador soon arrived and spoke to the Emperor of Blefuscu.

"Quinbus Flestrin must be tied up and returned to Lilliput," he said. "If you refuse to do so, it means war."

The Emperor of Blefuscu was thankful that I had not reduced his empire to slavery under the Lilliputians.

"I would love to do a favor for the esteemed Emperor of the Lilliputians, but I cannot. You can return home and inform him that we will both soon see the last of the monster. He is planning to return to his home and has found a way to do so."

When I heard this, I was more eager than ever to leave. Five hundred workmen began to make sails for my boat. They sewed together thirteen thicknesses of their strongest linen. I wove together twenty or thirty of their strongest ropes to make a single sturdy line. I found a great stone to serve as an anchor. I used lard from three hundred cows to grease the bottom of the boat. I cut down the tallest tree I could find to make a mast. After I roughly shaped it, I handed over to the Emperor's carpenters to smooth.

In the boat, I store the carcasses of a hundred butchered cattle and three hundred sheep, cooked by four hundred cooks. I also took thousands of loaves of bread and many casks of wine. I also took six cows and two bulls alive. If I could get them back to England and breed them, they would be a great curiosity. I took hay and grain to feed them on board.

I hoped to take a few of the people of Blefuscu, too. There were many who would have gone with me. They were eager to see the land I described, where everybody was a giant.

But the Emperor would not allow it. He had my pockets searched before I left and made me swear not to take any of his subjects with me.

After a month of preparation, I was ready to go. The Emperor of Blefuscu and the royal family all came out to see me off. I lay down on my belly to kiss his hand and the Empress's hand. He gave me fifty purses, each with two hundred *spurgs* in them, which were their tiny gold coins. He also gave me a full-length portrait of himself, which I put in my glove to keep safe.

Thousands and thousands of people came out to see me leave. On the 24th of September 1701, at six in the morning, I pushed my boat away from shore and left Blefuscu and Lilliput behind. I rowed a few miles into the sea, then caught a fair breeze and hoisted my sails. By six that night, I was long out of sight of the two small islands.

Near sundown, I spotted another island off to the east. I sailed toward it and found a bay where I could cast out my anchor. There didn't seem to be any people living on the island.

I took some food ashore and lay down to rest. I slept a few hours. A couple of hours before dawn I awoke and ate breakfast. I pulled up my anchor and set sail again, heading on the same northern course. I was glad I had saved my compass in my secret pocket.

I saw no land that day or the next. Finally, about three in the afternoon, I saw what I thought was a sail. Yes, it was! It was a ship!

She was headed to the southeast. I turned due east to try and catch up with her. I yelled, but the sailors could not hear me.

The wind was light. I put up all the sails I had and slowly gained on the ship. Finally they put up a flag and fired off a cannon to let me know they'd spotted me. I can't tell you how happy I was. Now I had hope of getting home, back to my wife and my darling children. I hadn't seen them in a year and a half.

About six in the evening of September 26 I finally caught up with the ship. I was overjoyed to see her flying the English flag.

She was a merchant ship returning from Japan. Her captain, John Biddel, was a very nice man and great navigator. He had about fifty sailors, including a man named Peter Williams, whom I had met on another voyage.

"Captain, I know this man," he said. "He's a decent fellow and a doctor. You can trust me on that."

"We're glad to have you aboard," said Captain Biddel. "How did you come to be sailing the wide ocean in that little boat? Where are you coming from?"

I told him all about Lilliput and Blefuscu and the things that had happened to me there.

"I'm afraid," he said to Peter, "that your friend here is crazy as a loon. The shipwreck he was in must have knocked him out of his senses."

"If you don't believe me," I said, "have a look at these."

I had put the living cattle and sheep into the pockets of my coat. Now I took them out and set them on his table. The captain and the others were amazed. Their eyes practically bugged out of their heads.

I showed Captain Biddel the picture of the Emperor of Blefuscu. I gave him two of the purses with the tiny gold coins. I said when we arrived in England I would give him a cow and a sheep as well.

We still had to sail all the way around the world. On the way, I fed my little cattle and sheep with sea biscuits that the captain gave me. It was not until April 13, 1702, almost two years after I had left home, that we landed back in England.

When I got back, I found that the tiny animals fared well on English grass. I had been afraid it would be too tough for them. I was able to breed more of them. The sheep gave such fine wool that they were in demand. I sold them for a great deal of money.

I swore that I would never go to sea again. I was happy just to be with my wife Mary and my children, Johnny and little Betty.

But you know how it is. If you have an urge to go places, you just can't sit still. After a few months, I felt that I had to get out and see more of the world. I had had such adventures in the land of Lilliput and Blefuscu, who knew what other wonders were waiting for me out there?

So I left part of my money with Mary and took the rest to trade with. I signed onto a merchant ship. It carried three hundred tons of cargo and was headed for India under Captain John Nicholas.

Guess what the ship was called. It was named the *Adventure*. And it would carry me to adventures all right, even stranger than the ones I had already had. But I'll tell you all about those in the next part of my story.

The End of the First Part

Part Two

A Voyage to Brobdingnag

1

Now, do you think that after all my misfortunes I was content to stay at home? No, I wasn't. Barely two months after I returned, I was off to sea again on the *Adventure*. We left on June 20, 1702 under Captain John Nichols. We were bound for the East Indies.

All went well at first. We made it around the Cape of Good Hope at the bottom of Africa. But we sprang a leak in our ship and the captain came down with a fever, so we had to sail into a port there and wait for almost six months. We started out again in March and sailed past Madagascar, a huge island in the Indian Ocean. That's when the trouble began.

A storm brought many weeks of fierce winds. The wind blew and blew, taking us far off course. The sailors had a hard time just keeping the ship from tipping over. We were blown where the winds seem to want us to go.

After three weeks of this we were lost. Even the oldest sailors on the ship said they had no idea where we were.

We still had food and I had managed to keep the crew in good health, but we were short of fresh water. We decided to go with the wind, hoping to reach land. If we didn't, we would die of thirst.

On June 16, 1703, after almost a year at sea, a boy in the crow's nest spotted land. The next day we came near a rocky beach. We didn't know if it was an island or a continent.

We dropped our anchor and the captain ordered a dozen men in a small boat to go ashore and look for water. I was always eager to find out about strange lands, so I asked if I could go, too.

The sailors found a small stream and began to fill casks with drinking water. I walked about a mile inland. There was something strange about the place. It was rocky, filled with large boulders. I didn't see any ordinary trees, only stalks of grass as tall as palm trees. I began to get nervous and headed back toward the creek. Coming over a rise, I saw that our men were already shoving the boat into the water. They were leaving me behind! They began to row as fast as they could toward the ship. Wait!

I was going to shout at them to let them know they had forgotten me. But at that same instant, I saw a huge monster in the shape of a man. I had never seen anyone of that size. He was as big as a mountain.

I watched him splash into the water. He waded up to his knees trying to catch our boat. But our men had a good head start and managed to reach the ship. The monster didn't dare go too far out because of the sharp rocks under the water.

The ship was quickly setting sail. The captain wanted to get out of there fast, and I could hardly blame him. But what about me?

The monster, who had waded in up to his waist, shook a fist at the ship. Then he turned and began to walk back toward shore. Seeing this, I ran and didn't look back. I wanted to get as far from that monster as possible.

Over a high hill I saw that there were farm fields. I began walking down what looked like a very wide highway. I knew I was passing through a wheat field, but I couldn't see anything because each stalk was forty feet high. Everything on this island was huge!

After an hour I came to an enormous hedge, at least a hundred and twenty feet high. Here and there, trees grew so high I couldn't even see their tops. A set of steps led into the next field. But they did me no good because each step was six feet high. I couldn't climb even onto the first one.

As I looked for a gap in the hedge, I heard the crash of gigantic footsteps. A group of monster men, each as huge as the one who had chased our boat, was coming over the steps. I ran and hid in the wheat field.

The first man stopped at the top of the steps and called to the others in a voice as loud as a fog horn. At first, I thought it was a clap of thunder.

Seven other monsters followed him. Each had a hook in his hand for cutting grain. The blades were as big as six of our large scythes.

I couldn't understand the words, but I got the idea that they were about to cut the grain in the field where I was hiding. I began to scurry away from them as quickly as I could. I had to fight my way through the wheat stalks, which were like small trees.

I made progress until I came to a place where rain had knocked down the wheat. It was as thick as a jungle. The end of each ear of wheat was so sharp it jabbed right through my clothes. The giants were gaining on me. I was lost!

I lay down and expected to die. I was sorry to leave behind my wife and two children with no husband or father. How stupid I had been to go looking for adventure again. I wished I was back in Lilliput where *I* was the giant.

Philosophers say nothing is large or small except in comparison to something else. I guess they're right. Here, I felt as tiny as an insect.

The farm workers were almost on top of me. I could hear the swish of their blades slicing the grain. In the next instant I expected to be either squashed under foot or cut in half by one of their hooks. Fear made me scream as loud as I could. "Stop!" I yelled. "I'm here!"

The huge creature stopped and looked around. My voice must have sounded to him like a tiny squeak. Finally, he looked down at me as if I were a small animal that might scratch or bite him. Very carefully, he picked me up by his thumb and forefinger. He raised me until I was a few yards from his eyes.

I did not struggle. I was sixty feet in the air and didn't want him to drop me. I clasped my hands and begged him to have mercy on me. He seemed to like my voice and knew I was speaking words, even if he couldn't understand them.

I groaned and looked at my sides to let him know he was pressing me too hard. He must have understood because he dropped me into his coat pocket and ran to his master, the first farmer I had seen.

This man took me and looked me over closely. He seemed surprised that I was wearing clothes. He set me down on all fours, but I immediately jumped to my feet. I walked slowly back and forth to show I didn't mean to run away. I tried as hard as I could to look like a man.

I took my hat off and bowed to the farmer. I removed my purse and motioned for him to put his hand on the ground. I poured out six large gold coins into his palm, but to him they were so small he didn't know what they were. He made a sign for me to put them back.

He spoke to me, but his voice was as loud as a clanking water mill and made as much sense. I wanted to cover my ears, it was so loud. I tried to talk to him in all the languages I knew, but he could make out nothing.

He laid out his handkerchief and motioned for me to lie on it. I did so. He wrapped me in it for protection and carried me home to his wife.

This lady, when she saw me, screamed and ran in circles, as if she had been startled by a mouse or spider. But seeing how gently I behaved, she soon became fond of me.

By now it was dinner time. A servant brought in a huge dish of meat about twenty-four feet across. The farmer, his wife, three children, and their old grandmother sat down for dinner. The farmer put me on the table, which was thirty feet high. I kept away from the edge, afraid of falling off.

The wife cut up a bit of meat and put it on a small plate with some crumbs of bread. I bowed and took my knife and fork out of my pocket. I was starving and the food tasted delicious. The wife poured some cider into their smallest cup, which held about two gallons. I took up the cup in both hands with some difficulty and toasted the lady's health.

Nobody could understand me, but they all laughed so loudly I thought the sound would burst my eardrums.

As I was walking across the table, I tripped over a crust of bread.

"Oh, no, perhaps the little thing has hurt himself," I imagined they were saying. They all seemed worried.

I took off my hat and waved it to show I was fine. "No harm done, ladies and gentlemen," I said. "I am perfectly fine."

As I came near the farmer, his son, who was about ten, grabbed me by the legs and held me so high I was afraid for my life. His father snatched me out of his hand and gave him a box on the ear that would have knocked over a whole troop of soldiers in my country. He was going to send him away, but I fell on my knees and begged his father to pardon him. I knew how mischievous children can be, so I didn't want the boy to become my enemy.

In the middle of dinner, I heard a noise that sounded like a buzz saw. I turned to see that the wife's favorite cat had jumped into her lap. She was petting it and it was purring. The cat yawned. You should have seen her huge teeth! She could easily have ripped me apart.

Though the wife held the animal fast, I was afraid the cat, which was bigger than I was, would jump at me and tear me apart with her claws. I backed as far away as I could.

I quickly thought better of my action. I have always heard that showing fear only makes an animal want to chase you. So I walked right up toward the cat, and she shrank back, as if she were afraid of me.

Still, I couldn't help being a little timid when four dogs came into the room. The largest of them was a mastiff. He stood as high as the table and was about four times as big as an elephant.

When dinner was almost done, a nurse brought in the family's youngest child, a baby about a year old. When the child saw me, she began to cry with a voice that carried five miles. Like all babies who see something new, she wanted to get hold of me.

Her mother, to stop the baby's crying, picked me up and held me toward her. The child grabbed me and immediately stuck my head in her mouth. I roared so loud that she let me drop. I would have broken my neck except the mother held her apron under me.

I noticed that this baby's skin was mottled and ugly. The skin of the adults was even worse. Giant hairs stuck out. They had pimples as big as dinner plates. They were blotched and greasy.

I remembered noticing that the skin of the people in Lilliput was much fairer and smoother than any I had seen. And I remembered one of my friends there telling me that I was a gross sight to him when he came near me. To him, my skin was like the skin of a wild boar, all bristles and blotches.

I realized now that it's all a matter of your point of view. I'm sure the people of Brobdingnag were no more ugly than the inhabitants of England, if you were to see them from the proper distance. But when you looked at them from my point of view, they were gross.

By the time dinner was over, I was very tired. The farmer's wife noticed this and put me on her own bed to rest. She covered me with a handkerchief, which was as big as the sail on a ship.

I slept for a couple of hours and dreamed of being back home with my family. When I awoke, I felt better. I saw that the bed was sixty feet across. I wanted to get down, but it was more than a twenty-foot drop to the floor. I tried calling out, but no one could have heard my voice, which must have sounded like a squeak to these giants.

As I was wondering what to do, two rats appeared. Sniffing, they came toward me. They were the size of large dogs, with tails six feet long. One of them even got his paw on my throat. Fortunately, I still had my dagger on my belt. I pulled it out and stuck it into his belly, killing him. His friend ran away, but I managed to wound him in the back.

I heaved the dead rat onto the floor. When the mistress of the house came in, she saw the blood on the bed and was afraid I had been hurt. When I pointed to the dead rat, she gave a cry of relief. She called the maid to pick the animal up with a pair of tongs and throw it out the window.

Through sign language, I said, "Dear Lady, I need to do something in private."

"Oh, I see," she said, also in signs. She giggled as she took me out into the garden. There I was able to hide myself behind some leaves so that I could pee. I don't like to mention things like this, but I am sure that readers will want to know all the details of my journey, and I can't leave anything out.

I was glad I had come to be taken in by these kind people. I was especially fond of the daughter of the house, who was about nine, a very smart little girl. Only she wasn't that little. She stood almost forty feet high. We soon headed off on a great journey, which I'll tell about in the next chapter.

2

This little girl and I became fast friends. She and her mother fitted up a cradle for me, put it inside the drawer of a cabinet and put that on a hanging shelf so that no rats could get at me. The girl made me seven shirts out of the finest cloth they had. To me it was like burlap, but I admired her needlework.

She also began to teach me their language. I pointed to objects and she told me the name of each. She was a good teacher and soon I could say a few words and be understood.

She called me *Grildrig,* which in their language meant "little fellow." I called her *Glumdalclitch,* which meant "little nurse." She was the most good-natured girl. Without her care and affection, I never would have survived in that land.

Word spread around the neighborhood that Glumdalclitch's father had found an unusual *splacknuck,* which in that land is a little rodent. But this *splacknuck* was shaped like a man and walked on two legs. It could speak a little language of its own, and even say a few words of their language.

A farmer who lived nearby was a great friend of the one I now called my master. When he came to visit, I put on a little show for him. I said, "How do you do," in his own language. I drew my dagger as I was told to and flashed it before him.

He was very nearsighted, so he had to lean close and look at me through his spectacles. His eyes looked so huge to me, like two moons, that I couldn't help laughing. The old fool took offense at this.

It turned out that he had one interest in life: money. His advice to my master was to take me to the market in the next town and charge folks to see me.

Glumdalclitch told me this later. She cried as she did so.

"I'm so afraid the vulgar oafs at the market might squeeze you to death or break off your arms or legs," she said. "I know you're an honorable little fellow and will not like being made into a show for the worst kind of people."

I tried to assure her that I could take care of myself, though of course it wasn't true.

"They said you would be mine to keep," she told me. "It's just like last year when they gave me a lamb. Then just when I learned to love it, they sold it to the butcher. They're always doing things like that."

Sure enough, the next day the farmer packed me into a little box with air holes in the sides. His daughter put the quilt of her doll's bed in it to keep me comfortable. She came along with us as we rode on horseback to town.

The horse went about forty feet with each step and each time he landed I was jolted up in the air. It was worse than being in a ship caught in a storm at sea.

It took us about half an hour to travel the twenty miles to the village. The farmer hired the *grultrud,* the town crier, to let people know that a strange creature could be seen at the Sign of the Green Eagle.

"He walks. He talks. He'll do some amazing tricks! Come one! Come all!"

The farmer put me on the table in the largest room in the inn. It must have been three hundred feet square. My little nurse stood close by on a low stool to care for me. My master allowed only thirty people into the room at once.

Glumdalclitch directed me to walk around. She asked me questions. I answered her and greeted the spectators and made a few speeches she had taught me.

"Draw your sword, Grildrig!" she said.

I would flash my dagger as if I was in a sword fight and all the people would laugh.

"March up and down!"

I marched and saluted as if I was a soldier in the army.

"No!" she yelled at a spectator who was reaching his hand toward the table. "Don't touch him. Nobody is allowed to touch. Stand back!"

A schoolboy fired a hazel nut at my head, thinking it a joke. It was as large as a pumpkin and would have knocked my brains out if it had hit me. The young rogue got a good whipping for doing so and was thrown out of the inn.

By the time market day was over, my master had made a good deal of money and I was as tired as I could be.

"He'll be on show next market day," my master told the many people who had not been able to get in to see me.

I didn't like this work at all. It took me three days to recover my strength. Not that I had any rest at home. Every day, people came from all around to see me at the farmer's house. The farmer was raking in plenty of money, but I was getting worn out. I could only rest once a week, on Wednesday, which was their sabbath.

"Here's what I plan to do with the little creature," I heard the farmer telling his wife one night. I could understand their language quite well now.

"I will take him all over the kingdom, visiting the largest cities and ending in the capital. We'll become richer than we've ever dreamed."

That was just what he did. In a few days he and Glumdalclitch and I headed off for the capital, which was 3,000 miles away. My little nurse carried me in a box tied around her waist. She had lined it with the finest cloth she could find and put her doll's bed inside.

We went from town to town and sometimes rode out to the homes of wealthy people in the country who wanted to see me. Now and then as we went along, Glumdalclitch took me out of the box so that I could see the passing countryside. It was quite a sight, hills grander than our highest mountains, huge lakes, towering trees. The streams seemed like raging rivers to me but the horse just trotted across them.

After ten weeks we had covered eighteen towns and many villages. He had also forced me to perform in countless private homes for the gentry of the land. Finally we reached the capital.

"What's the name of this city?" I asked my nurse. She was just as awe-struck as I was, since she had never been here before.

"It's called *Lorbrulgrud*," she said. "That means *Pride of the Universe*."

We set up in a large room that her father rented not far from the king's palace. He provided a table sixty feet across and put a fence around the outside so that I wouldn't fall off.

Ten times a day, I had to put on my show. People crowded in to see me. I worked so hard and long that I began to fall ill. Still I had to work. Never a day off except Wednesday. I knew that if I kept this up much longer, I would surely die.

But then a miraculous thing happened.

3

The more money my master made by showing me off, the more he wanted. All the farmer could think of was how rich he was getting. He made me work such long hours, I was steadily losing weight. I became a walking skeleton. The farmer didn't care as long as he was squeezing more money from showing me.

Then one day a *slardal,* a servant of the king's court, came and told the farmer that the Queen herself wanted to see me. Some of her ladies had attended the shows and had told her Majesty about me.

I was taken immediately to the palace and brought before the queen.

I fell on my knees and said, "Please, your Majesty, allow me the favor of kissing your royal foot."

Instead, I was lifted onto the table near her and she was gracious enough to hold out her little finger. I took it in both my arms and touched my lips to it.

She asked me about my country and my travels. I answered as distinctly as I could in her language.

"Would you, little man, be happy to live here in our court?" she asked.

I bowed low. "I would be proud to devote myself to you, your Majesty. But I am owned by a farmer."

"Would you be willing to sell this little creature?" she asked my master.

The farmer knew I would soon die because he was working me so hard. He agreed to let the queen have me for a thousand pieces of gold.

"I have one request, your Majesty," I said. "Let my good friend and nurse Glumdalclitch, who has been so kind to me, continue to be my companion and teacher."

"Very well, if her father agrees."

Of course he did agree. He was glad to have his daughter become a lady in the court of the king. Glumdalclitch herself was overjoyed.

The farmer wished us both good luck. I wouldn't answer him, though. I thought he had treated me quite badly.

"Why were you so cold to your former master?" the Queen asked me after he had gone.

"I guess I should be grateful he didn't knock my brains out as soon as he found me, your Majesty. But he nearly did kill me, showing me and making me do tricks all day every day. If he had not expected me to die soon, he would not have sold me so cheaply."

"I'm sorry he treated you badly."

"It doesn't matter now that I am under the protection of the Ornament of Nature, the Darling of the World, the Delight of her Subjects, the gracious Queen of Brobdingnag." I had learned from Glumdalclitch that this was the way to address and flatter the Queen.

"Well, I hope you will fare better in our court. To me, you are something very valuable, one of the greatest curiosities in the world."

"Your Majesty, I feel better already."

The queen was so happy with me that she took me in her hand and carried me to the King.

"What are you doing making a pet of a splacknuck?" he asked her, thinking I was one of those little rodents.

The Queen said I was something much more wonderful. She told how she had bought me from the farmer. She set me down and I bowed to the King.

"I think you've been duped, my dear," the King said to the Queen. "I think this is a little wind-up toy. It runs on clockwork. Ingenious, but hardly worth a thousand pieces of gold."

The Queen told me to explain myself to his Majesty. I briefly told him my story. The King was astonished that I could talk and answer questions.

Glumdalclitch, who could not bear for me to be out of her sight, was looking in the door. The Queen asked her to come in, and the girl said that my story was true.

The King sent for three great scholars who advised him at court. They examined me for quite some time. They studied me with a magnifying glass.

"Your Majesty, this little being is a real mystery," the first one said. "It seems impossible he could live in nature. He's not adapted for digging like a gopher. Nor for climbing trees, like a monkey. By his teeth we can tell he's a meat eater, but how he could ever kill an animal for food we can't figure out. Cattle are far too big, mice are too nimble."

"I think he's a dwarf," said the second.

"That's impossible," the third said. "No one's seen a dwarf so tiny. Why, the Queen's own dwarf is five times as big."

"In a word," the first philosopher said, "we don't know what he is."

"I can explain, your Majesty," I said. "I come from a land where there are millions of people just like me. Men and women both. Our cattle are of a size that we can eat. Our houses and cities are just the size that's right for us."

"That farmer told you to say this," the first scholar said. "There's no country on earth populated with such little creatures. It's impossible."

They all nodded their heads. Impossible.

"Whatever he is, he's an interesting and valuable creature," the King said. "He must be treated carefully."

So Glumdalclitch and I moved into rooms right there in the palace. The Queen appointed a governess to look after the girl and be her teacher. She asked her best carpenter to make me a room that would fit my size. This man worked for three weeks making me a bedroom sixteen feet square, with windows and closets and a bed. To them, it was a small box. The roof lifted up on hinges.

Every day Glumdalclitch took out my bedding to air. I had two chairs made from ivory and two tables and a cabinet. They put quilts on all sides of the room and the floor, so that I wouldn't be injured if it received a jolt.

The royal locksmith made me a lock for the door, to keep the rats out. It was the smallest he had ever made, though to me it was as big as you would find on a large gate. Tailors sewed clothes for me from their finest cloth. To me, it was like wearing a blanket because their cloth was so thick and coarse. Over time, though, I got used to them.

The Queen became so fond of me, she couldn't dine without me. My table was placed on top of her table, and I sat at her elbow. Glumdalclitch stood on a stool nearby in order to help me. The Queen's two daughters, the elder 16 and the younger 13, ate with us.

They loved to see me carve my meat and eat it. I can't say the same about watching them eat. To start with, their knives were as big as long scythes and could easily have sliced me in two. The Queen, who had a delicate stomach, would take as much food in her mouth as a dozen of our farmers could eat in a whole meal. She would eat a bird nine times as big as one of our turkeys in a single bite, bones and all. Then she would stuff bread in after it, hunks as big as two of our loaves. She washed it all down with a whole barrel of wine. I have to tell you, it made me sick to watch.

On Wednesdays, which I've mentioned is their sabbath, the whole royal family eats together. One of the princes was very curious about my country and I told him about how we live, our industry, our wars and our politics.

I was quite surprised when he laughed out loud and said to all the others, "Can you believe it? These little creatures have kings and noblemen just like we do. They have little nests they call houses and dress themselves up in fancy clothes. And they have politics and war, as if they were full-sized creatures. What a joke!"

They all thought this was very funny. I was mad as could be. I could not stand to hear England, the most wonderful and powerful country in the world, spoken of so rudely.

Of course, there was nothing I could say to answer him. In fact, I had so grown used to their point of view, that sometimes when the queen held me before her mirror, I would laugh at myself.

"What a tiny, silly little creature," I would say, pointing at my image. I was so used to seeing everything and everybody huge that I think if I saw others of my own size, I would probably have burst out laughing too.

The worst part of living there was having the Queen's dwarf around.

This man was the smallest in their whole kingdom. To me, he was about 30 feet tall. And whenever he saw me he would draw himself up and swagger.

He was always saying, "Excuse me, little fellow," or "What a pip-squeak you are!"

I would answer him with wisecracks. "Takes one to know one," or "Can I borrow some money, or are you short?"

One time, he got so mad at me that he snatched me up from the dinner table and threw me into a large silver bowl of cream. He ran away, leaving me there to drown. I might have, if I hadn't been a good swimmer. Luckily, Glumdalclitch saw me and saved me. My clothes were ruined.

The dwarf was sorry he did it because the Queen had him whipped and then made him drink the entire bowl of cream that he'd thrown me into. Afterwards, I was very happy to find out that she had sent him away from court.

Another problem was the flies. They were as big as birds in our country and were constantly buzzing around and annoying me. They would land on my nose and bite me. They smelled awful and their feet left behind sticky goo. The Queen saw nothing of this, to her they were just tiny pests. The people in Brobdingnag, I found, have poor eyesight.

One day, the Queen, noticing how fearful I was of the insects, asked me, "Are all the people in your land such cowards? Why, it seems you're afraid of a mere fly."

"You can't understand what it's like for me, your Majesty," I said. "One day Glumdalclitch gave me a piece of cake. Just as I was about to eat it, twenty wasps came into my room. They sounded louder to me than the drone of many bagpipes. I was terrified. I drew my sword and was able to kill four of them. The rest got away. You would be afraid too if you were attacked by such huge creatures."

She just laughed and said I was a silly creature, but she still liked me. I was embarrassed and wished that for once I could be the same size as everybody else.

The land of Brobdingnag is about 6,000 miles wide, twice as big as what our geographers think is the size of the New World. It is a mass of land, separated from the rest of the world by a range of high mountain. It borders the Pacific Ocean. The sea around it is so rough that the people are afraid to sail in it. So they have no contact with the rest of thee world.

They get fine fish from their streams and lakes, but the fish they find in the ocean are to them tiny. Sometimes they catch a whale, which they cook for the King. It's just big enough to fill a platter.

The country contains fifty-one cities and almost a hundred towns and villages. The capital, Lorgrulgrud, is built on a river that's almost fifty-four English miles wide. The King's palace is about seven miles around. The rooms are two hundred forty feet high. The Queen would allow Glumdalclitch and me to go around it in a horse-drawn coach as big as a church.

Something struck me when we went out among the common people. When I looked carefully, I could see lice crawling on their clothes. They were much larger than the tiny bugs that invest Englishmen, of course. Nasty creatures with snouts, they turned my stomach.

To make these trips easier, the Queen had another box made for me, smaller than the one I lived in and built very sturdily. The windows were covered with wire mesh to keep them from being broken. And on one side there were no windows but two handles that could be used to strap the whole thing to a person riding on horseback.

The ride was very rough, but the chairs and tables were screwed to the floor so they wouldn't move around. And I had a hammock I could lie in. I was used to being at sea, so I was able to put up with the swaying and tipping.

In this box, I could travel all over. I paid visits on great ladies and minsters of state. I went out to see the gardens, carried by a trusted servant. Usually Glumdalclitch came too. She didn't like to leave my care to anyone else.

I went one day to see their largest temple. The tower of it is about a thousand feet high. The walls are a hundred feet thick. They have huge statues of their gods and heroes.

Glumdalclitch liked viewing these sights, too. She had lived all her life in the country. Near the temple she found that a little finger of one of these figures that had fallen to the ground. It was about four feet long, but tiny to her. She wrapped in her handkerchief and carried it home in her pocket. Like most little girls, she liked to collect these kinds of trinkets.

The King's kitchen was about 600 feet high. The pots and kettles there were so huge that you wouldn't believe me if I described them. His horses are 60 feet tall, and he keeps 600 of them in his stables. When his militia ride out for a parade, it's a grand sight indeed.

The Queen did everything she could to make me comfortable. My life there would have been quite relaxing, except for the animals I encountered. I'll tell all about them in the next chapter.

5

There was a lovely garden in the palace. Glumdalclitch often took me out there to enjoy the outdoors. I had to be on the watch, though. Once, when she left me alone there, a violent shower of hail came. Each piece of hail was as big as a tennis ball. They gave me many cruel bangs all over my body. I was so bruised I had to stay in bed for a week.

Another time, while Glumdalclitch was walking with her governess and some ladies, a white spaniel dog came sniffing along. He picked me up in his mouth and ran straight to his master, who was the chief gardener. Fortunately, he'd been taught so well to retrieve that he carried me without hurting me or even ripping my clothes.

He set me on the ground and looked up at his master, wagging his tail. The gardener was a great friend of mine, so he was horrified to see what had happened. He got down on his hands and knees and asked me how I was. I was so shocked and out of breath I couldn't speak. He was worried and carried me to my little nurse. She had found me missing and was terribly afraid.

She scolded the gardener severely. But nobody told the Queen. They didn't know whom she would blame. As for me, I was glad. To be carried around in the mouth of a dog is nothing I'm proud of.

Oh, I had many dangerous encounters with animals. A big bird of prey once swooped down and tried to grab me. I was able to fight him off with my sword. Another time I fell into a mole-hole. I went down up to my neck. And I banged my shin once against the shell of a snail.

One day, the Queen, knowing that I had been on a ship, asked me if I could sail. I said I had learned enough of the craft to handle a boat quite well. She had a boat made for me to have fun in. She also had her men make a basin filled with water to sail in. It was like a horse's drinking trough, only it was three hundred feet long.

I could row this boat or put up a sail. If there was no wind, the Queen and her ladies would make one by waving their fans. Or they would order their servants to blow with their breath to make my boat go.

The servants changed the water in this trough every three days to keep it fresh. One time, a frog got into the pail that they brought. He hid until my boat was coming by, then climbed up onto it to rest. He was a huge and slimy animal, I could hardly stand the sight of him. He almost tipped my boat over before I banged him with one of my oars and forced him to hop out.

Another time I was resting in my box. Glumdalclitch was away for a visit. It was a hot day and she had left the windows of our rooms open. I was in my bigger box and also had the window open.

I heard a noise. I didn't see anything at first. Then I looked out and saw that a monkey had come into the room. In a second he was over near my box and looking curiously into the window. I retreated to the farthest corner of my room. He looked in at one window, then another. I didn't think to hide under the bed.

After peeping, grinning and chattering, the monkey finally saw me. He reached in with his paw and grabbed for me. I dodged him at first. Finally he caught hold of my coat and pulled me out. He was about the size of an elephant in our country.

He held me in his right paw. When I struggled, he squeezed me so tight I could hardly breathe. Better, I thought, to relax.

I think he thought I was a baby monkey. He cradled me in his arm and pushed out his lips at me.

At that moment, Glumdalclitch came in. Seeing her, the monkey climbed right out the window and up the side of the building. My little nurse was horrified. Her screaming alerted everyone in the palace.

The next thing I knew, the vile creature had carried me up to the very top of the roof. I was probably 1,500 feet in the air. If he had dropped me, I would have suffered a horrible death.

Servants ran for ladders. Glumdalclitch continued to scream in the courtyard below. Everyone came out to see.

The monkey was holding me in one arm the way you would hold a baby. With his other hand, he was trying to feed me with some filthy food that he'd been chewing on.

Some of those on the ground laughed. I was awfully embarrassed, but I could hardly blame them. It must have made a ridiculous sight.

"Let's hit that monkey with stones," a boy sad. "That'll drive him off!"

"Don't you dare!" Glumdalclitch cried. "He might let Grildrig fall!"

Now servants were climbing up the roof from all directions. Seeing himself surrounded, the monkey let me go and made a run for it. I grabbed a roof tile and held on for dear life. A gust of wind or my own giddiness might any moment make me lose my grip and fall.

Luckily, one of the Queen's footmen reached me in time. He put me in his pocket and climbed down the ladder. I was safe!

I fell down and vomited the awful stuff that creature had forced down my throat. Glumdalclitch took me home and put me to bed. I could barely get out for two weeks, I was so sick.

The King, Queen and all the members of the court asked about me every day. The King ordered the monkey to be killed and forbid any others ever to be kept in the palace.

Once I was better, Glumdalclitch took me out to the country to improve my spirits. It was a fine day and I was eager to stretch my legs and arms. Walking along a country path, I came to a very large plop of cow dung. Feeling quite frisky, I decided I would show off by jumping over it. I took a run and leaped. I almost made it.

Almost, but not quite. I splashed down in dung up to my knees. I had to wade the rest of the way and ended covered with filth. A footman tried to clean me off with his handkerchief. Glumdalclitch held her nose and told me I had to stay in my box until we returned.

Of course my little nurse had to tell the Queen what happened. And the footman told everybody. And soon everyone in the palace was laughing at my silliness.

6

After I had been on Brobdingnag many months, I began to need things that they couldn't supply me with. For example, I asked the King's barber to save me some suds which he scraped off his Majesty's face. From these I picked out forty or fifty of the barbs of the King's beard. I took a narrow piece of wood, made holes in it, and stuck these barbs through it. Some of them I had to scrape with my knife to fit. This made me a fine and useful comb to replace mine, which had gotten broken.

I asked the Queen's hairdresser to save me out some of the strands of her Majesty's hair. I used these to weave into seats and backs for two chairs. When I finished, they were better than the best caned chairs in England. I gave them to her Majesty as a present and she showed them to all her guests, who couldn't believe the fine workmanship.

"Show my ladies how you can sit on these adorable little chairs, Grildrig," the Queen said.

"I would do anything for you, your Majesty. But I cannot even think of doing what you ask. Why, to place that part of my body on the precious hairs that have adorned her Majesty's head? Never. Never, I say."

I even wove a purse out of the Queen's hair. It was about five feet long and had the Queen's name embroidered in the side. This I gave to Glumdalclitch.

"Why, thank you, Grildrig," she said. "It's lovely. Of course, it's too small to hold any coins. Maybe I can find some toys small enough to put in it."

The King loved music and often had concerts in the palace. He invited me to attend.

"I will be happy to, your Majesty. But the sound of your instruments is so loud that it pains my ears. I don't think all the drums and trumpets of our royal army band back home could even come close to it."

"What can we do to make it enjoyable for you?"

"If you place my box way back there in the corner, it will help. And, if you don't mind, I'll shut the windows and doors and draw the curtains."

When this was done, the music was quite nice. I still had to stick my fingers in my ears during the loudest parts, but I didn't tell the King that.

Once I mentioned to the Queen that I had learned to play the piano when I was a boy.

"You did? That's wonderful. You must play one of your English tunes for me and the courtiers."

I agreed, but it was easier said than done. The keyboard of their piano was 60 feet long. With my arms reaching wide, I could only reach five keys. To press them down, I had to hit them as hard as I could with my fist.

This is how I managed it. I got hold of two sticks of wood and padded the end of each with mouse skin. In front of the piano, I had them place a long bench. To play, I ran up and down, hitting the keys. The Queen wanted to hear a jig and I almost wore myself out trying to keep the time as I sprinted from one key to the other. Of course I couldn't play very well, but they all said it was a delight to hear this strange tune.

Many times I sat alone with the King and explained to him what life was like in England. He was a curious man and considered well-educated. But he had an awful ignorance about foreign countries.

"Our country is ruled by a king, just like yours," I told him. "We call him the King of England. He takes the advice of the Houses of Parliament." I described about the elections for the House of Commons and gave him a short account of the whole history of England.

"I don't think your system there is very sound," he said.

"Why not, your Majesty?"

"Because, as you describe the election of members of Parliament, it seems easy for a man to buy an election just by spending more than another man. That would not be allowed here. And your courts let anyone bring a suit, no matter how just it is. That's no good. Plus, a plaintiff might win a suit who doesn't deserve to just because he has a lawyer who's a skilled speaker. Do you call that justice?"

"Well, the system is not perfect, I will admit that."

"Not perfect? It's terrible. You say your King borrows money to carry on wars? That's silly. And that he keeps a large army always on the ready? Who are you so eager to fight? And this gambling you talk about. That's not how people should behave, especially young people."

"You do have a point there."

"My little friend, Grildrig, your description of this kingdom you call 'England' has convinced me that it is a place of ignorance, idleness, and crime. I hope that by traveling you have escaped many of the bad traits of your fellow Englishmen. But I can't help but conclude that the people of your country are a race of the most awful little vermin who have ever crawled on the earth."

7

I was burning up to hear the King talk about my wonderful country in such a way. I had described England truthfully, perhaps even playing up its good points. He talked as if it was the most terrible country on earth.

Of course I could not argue with him. He was the ruler of that land. Maybe because his country was so isolated, and because he had never visited other places, he could not understand much about our kingdom.

In hope of making a good impression on the King, I told him about an invention that had been discovered in our country about 300 years ago.

"It's a powder, your Majesty. A heap of it, if you put a spark to it, kindles in an instant. It explodes with a noise louder than thunder. What we do is to take some and put it into a hollow tube of brass. It blows a ball of iron out so fast that it can knock over a whole troop of soldiers."

"What? I've never heard of such an invention."

"That's not all. These balls, which we call cannonballs, can knock down a stone wall. They can sink ships. And if we put some of this powder inside an iron ball, it will blow up and throw splinters to all sides, killing people in the cities we are attacking."

"What you say is quite amazing. Are these things common in England?"

"Oh, yes. And I know all about the make-up of this powder. I can direct your workmen how to make some. And I can tell them how to construct the tubes -- cannons we call them. With these weapons, your power would be tremendous. You could defeat any army and command any city in your kingdom to obey your orders. I would gladly do it to repay your Majesty for all the kindness you've shown me."

"I am absolutely amazed at you, Grildrig! To think of such an inhuman thing! Why would I want to batter down walls or kill many men at once? I'm all for new inventions, but this is an evil one that I will never allow in Brobdingnag. Not as long as I live."

Well, that shows you how short-sighted that King was. No monarch in Europe would pass up a chance to be the absolute ruler over his subjects and over other nations. The King of Brobdingnag, I guess, could be excused because of his ignorance. He knew little about the ways of the world.

I asked him why, if he didn't believe in war, he kept an army?

"Brobdingnag has never been invaded," he told me. "Many years ago, however, the nobles tried to grab power from the King. They tried to enslave the people. We fought many civil wars. That's the worst kind of war there is, brother against brother. Finally, after many years, my grandfather put an end to the warring. We have a small army whose duty is to keep the peace."

One day he asked me how many books there were in England about government.

"Thousands," I told him. "We have many scholars who try to figure out the best ways to rule a kingdom."

"That's so unnecessary. Here we have very few. I rule based on common sense, reason, and justice. Our court cases don't drag on for months and years like you say yours do. They are over very quickly. All those scholars would be better off becoming farmers and growing something for people to eat."

Indeed, I knew that the education in that country was limited to morality, history, poetry and mathematics. They didn't study abstract ideas.

"No law in our country can have more words than there are letters in our alphabet," the King told me. They used only 22 letters, so that meant the laws were very brief. "The language is plain and simple. We don't need lawyers to tell us what the laws mean, as you say you do."

I learned more about their system by reading some of their books.

This was not so easy—they were 18 feet high and had pages that were as thick as pasteboard. To do it, I asked the Queen's carpenter to make me a set of stairs twenty-five feet high and fifty feet long. I would prop a book against the wall, then climb to the highest step to read the text, walking along as I did so.

When I finished one line, I would take a step down and read the next one. When I reached the lowest step and read the last line, I would heave the page over and climb back to the top to read the next one.

In one of these books I read the strange theory that very different men had lived in Brobdingnag in times of old. Many generations ago, the book said, the people there had been much larger, giants even. But today, because of the easy life they lived, the people had shrunk to their present, small size. The author even said that bones had been dug up that proved his theory.

Well, it was hard to imagine creatures who would be giants to these giants. It just shows you what strange ideas arise in every kingdom.

"You know what I could like, your Majesty?" I said to the King. "I have been in Brobdingnag for two years, but I've never traveled very far. I'm always curious to see new sights. I could think of nothing better than taking a tour of your kingdom."

"Very well," he said. He was a very agreeable man. "The next time her Majesty and I go on a visit to a distant part of the kingdom, I'll take you along."

"And don't forget my little nurse," I said.

"Of course, Glumdalclitch can come, too."

I couldn't wait to see more of this fantastic land. But it would be the start of a very dangerous adventure. I'll tell you all about it in the next chapter.

8

Before too long, the King planned to visit the southern part of his Kingdom. This was my chance to see this vast land. I asked the carpenter to cut a small hole about a foot square in the roof of my traveling box so that I could have air when I needed it or could shut it up with a piece of wood. I also had him fix the hammock more securely so that I didn't bounce around as much when my box was buckled to the waist of a man on horseback.

So off we went, bumping and jolting along, covering great distances. Soon we arrived at Flanflasnic, a city near the seaside. Glumdalclitch and I were both tired. In fact, my little nurse had taken quite ill. She had to stay in bed, her governess said.

"One thing I desire, now that we have come so far," I told Glumdalclitch. "That's to see the ocean. Remember, I'm a man of the sea. The sight of the waves and the smell of salt air is something I miss terribly."

"But you know I can't bear to have you leave my sight," she said. "Especially in this strange part of the kingdom."

"But what could happen?"

"You could get lost."

"Nonsense. I'll be fine. I'll just watch the waves for a while and return. I'll be perfectly safe."

"I don't know. I have a bad feeling that you'll come to harm if I let you go."

"Please, Glumdalclitch. I haven't seen the ocean in so long."

"Okay. But you must be very, very careful."

"Oh, I will."

She ordered the King's most trusted servant to carry me down to the sea. It was about a half hour walk before we reached the beach. I asked the young man to set my box down.

All the journeying had worn me out. As soon as I breathed in the sea air, I began to feel sleepy. I told the servant to let me rest. I lay in my hammock and listened to the waves. He went off looking for birds' eggs among the rocks.

I guess I fell asleep, because suddenly I was jolted awake. It felt as if someone had yanked on the ring on the roof of my box. I rose off the ground, then kept going! I was flying!

The first motion had knocked me out of the hammock. I leaped up and ran to the window. Now I was moving along quite smoothly, mounting higher and higher into the air. I could see the beach below, the waves crashing in. What could possibly be carrying me?

I soon guessed at the truth. An eagle had picked up the box and was carrying it off. He must have smelled me inside and was planning to drop the box onto the rocks from a great height. The box would break open and let him eat me up. I had seen sea gulls do the same thing to clams and crabs.

Yes, I could hear his wings beating. He must have been huge. I had never been so high before. At first I cried out, "Let me go! Help!"

Then I stopped shouting. I knew that if he did let go of me, I would be killed.

Now I heard him flap his wings faster and the box began to sway and toss. I heard the beating of more wings. Other eagles, I guessed, were trying to take the box away. They were fighting over me.

Then, suddenly, I was falling! I fell down, down, down! I was speeding so fast I could hardly catch my breath.

Then, splash! A roar as loud as Niagara Falls filled my ears. Everything went dark. I had fallen into the sea.

I felt myself going down into the water. Then after a minute I rose up again. My box was made very strong, with iron braces at each corner, so it survived the shock. I found myself floating in the water. The carpenter had done a good job constructing it. A little water oozed in here and there, but I patched up the cracks as well as I could. I could look out my windows and see fish.

But how could I get out? I climbed up to the ceiling and opened the panel that covered the hole. That let some air in at least, but it was too small for me to crawl through.

I wished then that I had never left my dear Glumdalclitch. I couldn't stop thinking about the distress my little nurse would feel when she found out what happened. The Queen would be furious at her. Her Majesty would blame Glumdalclitch for letting me be lost. The poor girl would have to go home in disgrace.

Of course, my own problems were a lot worse than that. I expected at every moment that my box would be smashed against the rocks. Or a big wave would come and tip it over.

Through the windows I saw only water. If one pane of glass were to break, my box would be flooded and I would sink straight to the bottom. I was glad the carpenter had put the wire screen over the windows. That was all that kept them from shattering.

The top of the box was far too heavy for me to lift, or I would have climbed out and sat on the roof. At least then I would have had a chance to escape if it sank. I hated being shut up and helpless inside.

I knew I could not survive long. In a day or two I would die a miserable death from cold and hunger. I drifted on the sea for four hours, expecting and even wishing every moment to be my last.

Then a funny thing happened. I began to imagine that my box was being towed through the water. I looked out the windows, but could see nothing. But yes, I was moving! I could see seaweed streaming past me.

What could be pulling me? Was it the eagle again? Was it a giant fish?

I climbed up on the table and brought my mouth as close as I could to the air hole in the ceiling. I yelled for help as loudly as I could. I called out in every language I knew. I tied my handkerchief to a stick and stuck it through the hole, waving it. Oh, if only a boat or ship were nearby. If only sailors came by who could see that the box held a human being.

After an hour, I felt the box clunk up against something. The jolt knocked me down. I had hit a rock, maybe. I heard noises but could see nothing.

Something was lifting me up. I could see that my box had risen about three feet out of the water. I waved my stick through the roof again. I called, "Help! Help!" until I was hoarse.

Then I heard someone shout back. I was overjoyed. A voice was calling through the hole in the ceiling. In English!

"If there's anybody in there, speak up!" the voice said.

"It is I, Lemuel Gulliver! I'm an Englishman. I've had an awful time of it. Get me out of here!"

"Don't worry, your crate is fastened to our ship. The carpenter is coming to cut a hole in the top and get you out."

"Don't bother. Just put your finger through the ring on top and lift the box out of the water. Then bring it into the captain's cabin and unfasten the lid."

"What are you talking about? Are you crazy? No man could lift that hulk out of the water."

I could hear others laughing. I didn't realize that I was back among people who were no taller than I was.

The carpenter came and sawed a hole about four feet square. He let down a small ladder. I climbed out and was pulled onto the ship.

The sailors asked me a thousand questions, but I was too weak to answer. I couldn't get over seeing so many pygmies. That's what they looked like to me after spending so long in a land of giants.

The captain, Mr. Thomas Wilcocks, saw that I was about to faint. He took me into his cabin and gave me a drink.

"Captain," I told him, "I have some valuable furniture in my box, a hammock, bed, chairs and table. Bring the box in here so that you can save them." I was still thinking that he was a giant.

"We'll see about that. You get some rest, Mr. Gulliver. You need it."

I lay down and was soon asleep. While I slept, the sailors recovered some of my things, then let the box sink to the bottom.

When I awoke, I felt much better. The captain gave me supper and told me how I had been found.

"At noon we saw what we thought was a ship. I changed course to make for it, hoping to buy some biscuits. When we got closer, I sent out some sailors in the longboat to take a closer look. They came back, saying they had seen a floating house. I went out myself and we attached a rope to the big pipes on the side of your -- whatever it was."

"It was a very fine box constructed by a carpenter of Brobdingnag."

"Well, anyway, we fastened it to the ship and tried to pull it up using ropes and pulleys. But even with every sailor hauling, we could only raise it two feet."

"Did you see any very large birds flying around earlier?"

"Now that you mention it, one sailor did report seeing several eagles way off in the sky. But so high, the man couldn't tell how big they were. I thought it odd, since we're a good 300 miles from any land."

"Oh, no, you're wrong there. We're quite close to land. I was on land only few hours ago. My little nurse, she got sick. And I wanted to see the ocean. And the boy went hunting eggs. And this bird came and lifted me up. And then--"

"That's all right, Mr. Gulliver. You need some more rest. We've got a cabin fixed up for you."

"I'm well rested now, thank you, captain."

"Well, your talk is pretty wild. I think you've been under a strain."

"No, captain, my head is entirely clear."

"Tell me this. Have you been convicted of some terrible crime? Did some prince set you to sea in that box as punishment?"

"No, I beg you to let me tell you my story. You'll know I'm telling the truth."

He was a patient man and he listened to my tale, from the time I left England until the moment that I came aboard his ship. He sensed that I was telling the truth.

To prove it, I asked him to have his men bring in my chest. I opened it and showed him what I had inside. There was the comb I made from the King's beard. There were some needles, almost two feet long. I had the stings I had taken from the wasps I killed, and some of the Queen's hair, and a ring that her Majesty had given me. She had worn it on her little finger, but it fit easily over my head like a collar.

I tried to give the captain this ring as a reward for saving my life, but he would not accept it. I did give him a tooth that a dentist had removed from the mouth of one of the Queen's footmen. I had had it cleaned and kept it. It was a foot long, bigger than an elephant's tooth.

"One thing I would ask of you, Mr. Gulliver," he said. "Please don't speak so loudly. I'm not hard of hearing."

"I'm sorry, captain. For the past two years, I've had to practically shout to be heard. Talking to a person in Brobdingnag was like talking to someone who's up in the top of a church steeple."

I confessed another odd thing to him. "When I first came aboard your ship, I thought your men were the most contemptible little creatures I had ever seen. I had grown so used to people who were of tremendous size."

The captain told me that he had been in Southeast Asia, but had been driven off course by a strong wind. Now he was sailing west.

We went around the Cape of Good Hope, entered the Atlantic Ocean and headed northward for home. I arrived back in England on June 3, 1706, nine months after I was rescued.

As I made my way toward my home, I couldn't help marveling at how small the houses were, how tiny the cattle and the people. It almost seemed to me that I was back in Lilliput. I was afraid of stepping on the folks in the road, and once or twice I called for them to watch out. They gave me odd looks, all right.

My wife Mary, and my children Johnny and Betty, were overjoyed to see me. I had been away so long, they didn't know what had become of me.

"One thing I ask, my husband," Mary said when I had told her all that had happened to me. "Don't go to sea again. You've had enough adventures to last you a lifetime. From now on, just stay at home with us."

I wish I had listened to her advice. I didn't. But that will be the subject of my next tale.

The End of the Second Part

Part Three

A Voyage to Laputa

1

Yes, you would think that I had seen all of the world that any man could want to see. And a lot more. I had come so close to death so many times, I should have been content to put my feet up and live the easy life with my wife and children. And that's just what I planned to do.

But travel gets into your blood. Only ten days after I arrived home, I was visited by Captain William Robinson. He was commander of the ship *Hope-well*. I had served as surgeon on another ship of his, and we had become close friends.

"I am glad to find you in good health, Lemuel," he said.

I told him about my trip to Brobdingnag.

"My, what a wonderful tale," he said. "Almost hard to believe it's true. You are positively the most intrepid traveler I have ever met, Lemuel. You should write an account of your journeys."

"Perhaps I will someday."

He came back to my house often. We traded stories of the times we had spent at sea and in distant lands. His tales were nearly as strange as mine.

"I'm headed out to the East Indies myself," he told me. "I'll be leaving in two months. It looks to be a profitable venture. Yes, sir, there's much money to be had. And something else, too."

"What's that, William?"

"Adventure!"

We talked about where he was going and the interesting places he would visit. Finally, he came to the point.

"Lemuel, I'll pay you twice your usual salary to come along as my ship surgeon. I'm sure I couldn't get a better one. And you can be my co-captain as well. Why, you know as much about sailing as anyone."

"That's a tempting proposal, William."

"I need you," he said. "You're the only one I know who's familiar with those parts of the world. You'll be a valuable addition to my crew."

I was already longing for a new adventure. I could not resist his offer.

It took me a while to convince Mary. She was not eager to have me go.

"Darling," I argued, "I'll be able to make enough money on this one trip that you and the children will be set for life when I return. I'll never have to go to sea again."

"Well, that does make it seem like the right thing," she said finally. "And I know how you love to travel. So, yes, Lemuel, I give you my permission. Go and seek your fortune."

We set out on August 5, 1706. It wasn't until the next April that we arrived on the coast of India. A good many of our sailors had taken sick, so I thought it better to wait there three weeks until they improved. Then we sailed to Southeast Asia.

"The goods we need to buy are not ready yet," Captain Robinson said. "It's likely to be a few months. I have a plan for you, Lemuel."

"What's that?"

"I know you won't want to stay cooped up here that long. I suggest we purchase a smaller sailing ship, a sloop perhaps. We'll load it with trade goods. You can sail it as a full-fledged captain. I'll give you part of the crew -- a dozen men, let's say. Take it around the islands here abouts and trade with the natives for spices, tea, even gold. You'll no doubt make a pretty penny. And perhaps have some adventures as well."

"That's a wonderful idea, William. Let's do it."

We purchased a sloop and I headed out. I was determined to make a lot of money to bring home to Mary. But luck was not with me. We ran into a terrible storm and were driven north, far off course. For ten days we struggled just to keep the small ship afloat in the towering waves.

Finally the weather cleared. Then what do you think happened? We were spotted by pirates. They chased us but we had no hope of escaping. Our sloop was too heavy with all the cargo we had aboard.

"They're sure to overtake us, men. Don't try to fight. We're far out-numbered and it will only mean our deaths."

Sure enough, the pirates caught us and climbed aboard.

While they were searching our ship to see what they could steal, I noticed that one of them was a Dutchman. I spoke Dutch well because I studied medicine in Holland, so I said, "Please have mercy on us. We're fellow Europeans, after all."

"Mercy?" he roared. "I would rather tie you back to back and throw you into the sea."

The captain of the pirates was Japanese, but he too spoke a little Dutch.

"This Dutchman tells me we should kill the lot of you," he said to me. "But I do not think it right to murder helpless men."

"What will you do with us?"

"Your men, we will hold them as prisoners. Later, maybe we'll give them the chance to join us. I don't think any will refuse. As for you, we have something different in mind for you."

The pirates took over our sloop and transferred my men onto their ship as prisoners.

They set me adrift in a canoe.

"We are being generous to you, Englishman," said the pirate captain. "We leave you with a paddle, a sail, and four days worth of food. Good luck."

He laughed and the rest of the pirates joined him. They knew that I had no chance. There I was in the middle of an unknown ocean. If I was not drowned in a storm, I would soon starve to death.

I drifted away and soon the pirates and my own sloop were out of sight.

I took out my spy glass and looked around at the empty sea. I could see nothing in any direction.

I put up the little sail and let the boat sail with the wind. I had no idea where I was headed.

Every few hours I gazed around with my telescope. Each time I saw nothing but water and sky.

But after many hours, staring to the south, I thought I spotted something. At first I wasn't sure. Then, yes, yes, it was land. Could it be an island? It was!

I turned the rudder and set off in that direction. It seemed to take forever but I finally came to a group of islands. I went ashore and collected some birds' eggs from among the rocks. I made a fire of dried seaweed and roasted the eggs. I ate nothing else. I knew I would have to make my food last.

This island was nothing but rocks, so the next day I sailed toward the next one. Sometimes I used my sail and sometimes my paddle. But when I arrived at that island, I found it as barren as the other. So I moved on to the next, and the next and the next. All I found were rocks, stones, and boulders.

The next day, I headed for the fifth and last island. It was farther off than the others and took more than five hours of sailing and paddling. I landed near a small creek. I found that this place too was nothing but rocks. Only a few tufts of grass grew here and there. I couldn't have been more discouraged.

I found a few more eggs and started a fire with my burning glass, focusing the sun's rays on some dry grass. I cooked my eggs and made my bed in a cave, lying on grass and seaweed.

The next day I was feeling very blue. How would I ever get off this barren island? Where would I go? I knew there was not enough food here to keep me alive long. I wandered among the rocks, under the hot sun, feeling sorry for myself and wishing I had never left home.

Suddenly, it grew very dark. It was if the sun had been blocked out. A great shadow had moved across the sea and was lying across the island. I thought it was a cloud at first. But it was much thicker than any cloud. Its shadow was almost as dark as night. It hid the sun for about seven minutes. What was it?

As it drew closer I could see that it was something solid. The bottom was smooth and flat. The reflection from the water sparkled off the material, whatever it was.

Slowly this giant thing drifted downward. When it came even with me, about a mile away, it stopped. I took out my spy glass. Through it I could see people! They were moving up and down the sides of this massive thing.

I had never seen anything like it. I had the wild hope that this might be my means of escape. But how? More likely, I was dreaming.

But I knew I wasn't. I was wide awake, no question about it. I was utterly astonished. How could an island be floating in the air? One with men on it. They seemed to be steering it and making it move up and down. They could also make it stand still, as it was now.

Through my telescope, I could see that people were sitting near the edge of the island fishing. They had long poles and lines that dropped all the way down into the water.

I waved my cap and my handkerchief and yelled to them. Soon a crowd of them gathered at the side and pointed toward me. Four or five men ran up the stairs that led down to the edge of the island and disappeared.

More and more people came to look at me. The ones nearest me were dressed in fine clothes, as if they were noblemen. The island slowly moved closer. When it was about a hundred yards away, I knelt down and held up my clasped hands to show that I needed help badly.

Finally one of the noblemen called out to me in a language that sounded like Italian. I answered in that language, yelling, "Please! Please, help me!"

But neither of us could understand the other.

The flying island came even closer. The men let down a rope with a seat attached. I climbed into it, sat down and held on. They hoisted me up with pulleys. I was off on a new adventure!

2

When I stepped onto this strange island, I found myself among a group of the oddest people I had ever seen. Their heads all leaned either to the right or to the left. Their eyes turned inward. Their clothes were covered with suns, moons and stars, along with images of fiddles, flutes, guitars, and trumpets.

Each of the noblemen had a servant with him who carried a little balloon on a stick. He used this to flap gently against his master's mouth and ears from time to time.

I didn't understand the reason for this then, but I later found out that the people there were very dreamy. If they didn't have a flapper to remind them to listen or speak, they wouldn't be able to get along in the world. Sometimes the flapper would flap the man's eyes to remind him not to walk off a cliff or into a ditch.

The problem was, they were always getting lost in their own thoughts. Sometimes they seemed to forget that I was there, until their flappers reminded them.

They took me before the King, who sat in a room filled with globes and spheres and mathematical instruments. He had two flappers. One of them flapped his eyes to remind him to look at me.

The King then said some words, perhaps welcoming me to this kingdom. A flapper flapped my ear to get me to listen. I, of course, didn't need any such reminder. I tried to answer him, but he didn't understand anything I said.

But I found that hospitality was something these people were very proud of. They took me to a comfortable room. Soon I was having a fine dinner with some of their important noblemen.

The food was as odd as everything else in that place. The mutton came in the shape of a triangle. The beef was square. They served a piece of duck in the shape of a fiddle. The pudding was a spiral.

After dinner, a man came to teach me the language. He had a pen and paper and made a list of words and showed by signs what they meant. I was soon able to say a few short sentences. He showed me books that had figures of the sun and moon and stars. He talked a lot about musical instruments.

He told me the name of the floating island was Laputa.

Soon a tailor came. "I'm to measure you for a new suit of clothes." He took my height only, then made a lot of mathematical calculations.

When he returned a week later, he brought me a very ill-fitting suit. The sleeves were so long I had to turn them up, but the pants left my shins bare. I didn't mind it too much, because everybody in that kingdom was dressed like that.

I came to understand that this island was only part of the King's realm. During the next four days we slowly glided over a mass of land. This was Balnibarbi, the part of the kingdom that was on solid earth.

"The King moves around from one city to another on Balnibarbi," one of the noblemen told me. "That's how he keeps track of what's going on in his territory. At each city, we send down for food and wine and draw it up using pulleys."

Finally, we came to hover above the capital, which they called Lagado. It was a rundown and old-fashioned looking city, at least from what I could see up on Laputa.

Mathematics and music, those were the only things these people ever thought of.

"Look at that beautiful woman," said the man who was teaching me their language. "She's shaped just like a parallelogram."

"That meal was as delicious as a string quartet," another might say.

"What a positively geometrical day," another would comment.

The people of Laputa were not good at building, or at anything else, for that matter. Their houses leaned over and were always in danger of collapsing. Everything they made, they made badly.

They were always talking about astronomy

"What do you think about the sun?" was a question that people asked all the time.

"I'm afraid we might crash into it and burn up," another would re-mark.

"There's a comet approaching," his friend would say. "We're likely to be scorched by the tail."

Every morning, when they got up, they consulted with their as-tronomers about the sun's health.

"Did it rise on time?"

"How did it look?"

"Is it as bright as yesterday?"

They sometimes spent half the day talking about it.

Some of the women of this land -- maybe they were smarter than the men -- didn't like all this silliness. I was told about a very rich lady of the King's court, the wife of the prime minister. Once she went down to Lagado. For her health, she said. But she didn't come back for months. They found her living in a filthy, rundown inn. She was wear-ing rags, but she had no wish to return to the flying island.

They brought her back, but soon she left again, taking all her jewels with her. She was never seen again.

One of the things that puzzled me, of course, was how in the world this island could fly. I was soon to find out the answer to this mystery.

3

The Flying Island of Laputa is an exact circle four and a half miles across. It's three hundred yards thick. On the bottom, it's made of very hard stone. On top of that is ordinary dirt.

The land slopes toward the center, so that all rivers and streams flow into four large ponds there, each about half a mile wide.

"Why don't they overflow?" I asked one of the astronomers.

"The sun evaporates the water," he said. "Besides, if it gets too wet, the King can just raise the island above the clouds to escape the rain."

In the center of the island is a deep pit, fifty yards across, called the *Flandona Gagnole,* or Astronomer's Cave. This is where the astronomers keep all their instruments and telescopes. We also have in here the object that is the secret of the Flying Island."

"What's that?" I asked my guide.

"It's a huge magnet. It measures six yards long and three yards thick. It's suspended on pivots so that we can move it easily, with just the touch of a hand."

"But how does it make the island fly?"

"You see, one end of a magnet attracts," the astronomer said. "The other end repels. Any fool knows that. So, if we tip the attracting end of the magnet a bit toward the earth, the whole island goes down. If we point the repelling end downward, Laputa rises. If we set the magnet at an angle, the island moves sideways. When it's exactly horizontal, we simply stand still."

"That's quite amazing," I said.

"It's all purely scientific and mathematical," he said. "The island can travel to any part of the kingdom. We can go as high as four miles up in the sky. After that, there's not enough repelling power."

He told me the magnet was under the care of the astronomers.

"These men are very skillful and highly mathematical. They've developed telescopes that can see ten thousand stars."

"Very impressive," I said. "Our astronomers back home can see only three thousand."

"Well, our telescopes are very advanced. We've detected two moons revolving around Mars. And we've discovered ninety-three comets whizzing through the solar system."

"How does the King of Laputa rule his empire if he never comes down from the Flying Island?" I asked him.

"Sometimes," he said, "a town will rebel against his Majesty. Maybe the people don't want to pay their taxes. The first step is to move the Laputa over the town and its surrounding land. That puts them in the shade and prevents rain. Their crops whither and they never see the sun. Usually, they submit quickly."

"What if they don't?" I asked.

"Sometimes we have to throw great rocks down on them. They, of course, have no defenses except to hide in their basements. We do a lot of damage, smashing in their roofs and all."

"Do they then submit to the King?"

"Not always. Sometimes they are very stubborn. In that case, we can make the island drop down directly on top of them. That destroys both houses and men. Fortunately, we usually don't have to go so far. The King doesn't like to resort to an action that destroys his own kingdom. And there's another reason as well."

"What's that?"

"Some of us are worried that crashing the island onto the earth could cause it to crack. You never know. We don't like to take the chance. That reminds me of the great rebellion of the people of Lindalino."

"What's Lindalino?"

"It's the second biggest city in the kingdom. The people there rose up against their governor and locked the gates of the city. They built four large towers at the corners of the city."

"What happened then?"

"We flew the Island over them, blocking the sun and rain. But they had food stored and a river ran through the town, so they could get water. Next we went to the edges of the island and threw stones at them. But they hid underground and in their strongest buildings."

"What did you do?"

"His Majesty could not tolerate such rebellion. He ordered the island to be lowered as a warning that he would smash the city. But when we tried to descend, we began to sink much too quickly. We were losing control of Laputa and had to pull it up. One of us lowered a small magnet on a rope and found out the cause. The magnet was pulled toward the closest tower. That told us there must be giant magnets inside each tower. They could stop us from attacking them. If we approached too closely, we would be trapped."

"How did you defeat them?"

"We didn't. The King had to give in to the demands of the people of Lindalino. It was a sad day, but we had no choice. No choice at all."

All this talk about the kingdom below, which I could see from Laputa, made me want to go down and explore for myself. In the next chapter, I'll tell you what I found there.

As I said, I was anxious to visit the land below us. I had gotten tired of talking with the silly people on the Flying Island of Laputa. So I finally convinced the King to let me go down.

On February 16 they lowered me by rope from the island down to the mainland. As I've said, this land below is called Balnibarbi and the main city is Lagado.

It felt good to have my feet on solid land again. I was dressed like a native and could speak their language. I had a letter of introduction to one of the Lords who lived there, a man named Munodi. He let me stay in his house and treated me very kindly.

The city of Lagado is about half the size of London. The people walk very quickly through the streets, looking wild and dressed in rags. Everything is rundown and in ruins. We walked into the country and saw fertile land, but it was very poorly farmed.

Lord Munodi was an important person there and had once been governor of Lagado.

"I have never seen a more disorderly and wretched place," I told him.

"You don't understand our ways. Tomorrow I'll take you out to my own estate."

We traveled the next day into the country. I saw no crops planted. All the houses needed paint or were falling down.

Then everything changed. We entered an area where there were vineyards full of grapes and meadows planted with crops.

"This is my farm," Lord Munodi told me. "All my countrymen hate me and laugh at me because I'm so old-fashioned and weak. Maybe they're right."

His house was beautiful, with fountains, gardens, walks and orchards. I told him how lovely it was.

"I'm thinking of tearing it all down," he said.

"Why would you do that?"

"This style went out of fashion years ago. I want to be more up-to-date. Then people won't make fun of me and I may gain favor with his Majesty again."

After dinner, he told me a little of the history of his country.

"It used to be that all the farms were like mine," he said. "Then about forty years ago, some people from here went to Laputa for a visit. They came back and told us we were doing everything wrong. They started an Academy and proclaimed a new day. New rules, new methods of farming, new tools and instruments came in. Everything began to be like it is in Laputa. You've seen the result."

"Why did people go along with it?"

"They said with the new methods, one man could do the work of ten. A building could be built in a week and would last forever. Crops could be harvested at any season."

"But that's clearly not true."

"No. They say it's because these projects haven't been completed. The whole country lies in ruins and waste because of their methods. But they're always coming up with still newer plans. When those are done, we will reap the benefits. So they say. They mock anyone who is old-fashioned, like me."

"That's a shame," I said.

"I guess it's progress."

I told him I would like to meet the people who had started the Academy. He said he would be glad to take me.

The Academy was about three miles away, on the side of a hill. Along the way, we passed a great mill, which stood in ruins.

"What's that?" I asked

"I had a water mill there, driven by a strong river, for milling my grain. The men from the Academy thought it would work better if it was up there on that hill. They destroyed my mill and built a new one up there. But to get the water to it, they had to dig a long canal and use pipes and engines. A hundred men worked on it for two years, but it never operated. They blamed me for the failure."

We walked quite a way before we came to the Academy. It was a large ruin of a building on the hillside. Lord Munodi told me, "I've arranged for a friend of mine to take you in and introduce you. The men of the Academy don't like me much."

I went with his friend. I was very eager to see the wonders of the Academy. All my life, from when I was a boy, I've loved inventions and new things.

5

I spent the next few days in the Academy. The Warden showed me around and seemed very glad to have a visitor from a distant land. He was very proud of the work they were doing there.

He introduced me to an old man, all sooty and ragged, with a long beard.

"This man is one of our top scientists," he said.

"What are you working on?" I asked the scientist.

"I've spent eight years finding a way to get sunbeams out of cucumbers," he told me. "Cucumbers soak up a lot of sun. I extract it and put the sunbeams in glass jars. Then I let them out when the weather is cold."

"How is your work going?"

"Oh, very well indeed. In a few years I should have enough sun to supply the Governor's garden. At a very reasonable cost, too."

"Could I see some of the jars?"

"Well, right now, my stock is quite low. You could help me out, though. The price of cucumbers this year has gone up terribly. If you could give me some money, it would be a great help."

I gave him a small amount. Lord Munodi had furnished me with some, telling me, "You'll need it."

We passed into another room where there was a horrible stink in the air.

"Pretend not to notice the smell," the Warden said. "You'll offend the scientist."

The man here was the oldest in all the Academy. His face and beard were yellow and he was filthy. When I was introduced, he gave me a hug. Phew! It was something I could have done without.

"I'm working on an exciting project," he said. "I am inventing a way to turn human excrement into food. All I have to do is to remove the digestive juices and get rid of the smell."

He said the Academy was generous enough to give him a whole barrel of excrement for his experiments every week.

Next, I met an architect who was making up a new way to build houses.

"With my method," he told me, "the builder starts at the roof and builds down. It's the natural way, really. Bees and spiders do it."

The next scientist was a blind man who was working on a way to mix paint. He taught his apprentices, who were also blind, how to determine the colors by smelling and feeling them. They were usually wrong, but they didn't know it.

In another room, an inventor was working on a way to plow the ground using hogs.

"You simply take nuts, acorns, and other things pigs like to eat. You bury them six inches apart in a field. Then you let loose six hundred hogs. They will root up the ground in a jiffy. And they'll manure it with their dung at the same time. That's a bonus."

"Does it work?"

"Well, the hogs are rather expensive, it's true. And they don't plow very well. But we're working on it. Yes, sir, we only need a little more time. And a little more money."

The next room was filled with cobwebs. The Warden introduced me to a scientist there who was trying to use the webs to make cloth, just like silk. Even better, he planned to dye the cloth by feeding the spiders with different color flies. He wasn't making much progress.

The last scientist I met here was known as the Universal Artist.

"He has invented so many things, we can hardly keep track," the Warden told me. "He has improved life in our land immensely."

Fifty men were at work in his laboratory. The Universal Artist showed me a few of the projects they were working on.

"Here is my idea to condense air into a dry, solid substance," he said. "Powdered air. Very valuable."

"And what's this man doing?"

"He's working on taking marble, which is beautiful but very hard, and turning it into soft pillows. And this man is trying to find a way to take the chaff from the grain and use it for seed. That will save a lot of money. And here we are working on a great project to breed sheep with no wool. It'll let them stay cool in the summer. And here . . ."

He showed me a lot of other projects, but most of them I didn't understand.

In another room, I saw a group of young boys sitting around a very complicated machine.

"This is a wonder," the Warden said. "It's my own invention, a machine that allows the most ignorant person to write about any subject. Philosophy, poetry, law, mathematics, you name it. They can compose an interesting essay without any study or knowledge. Any fool can use it."

"How does it work?"

"The machine has words written on the sides of these beads, which you can see are lined up in rows. As the machine turns, it rearranges the words. Then the boys read them off to see if they make an interesting combination. Sometimes the words form a phrase, even a whole sentence. When that happens, they write it down. Then the machine turns again, bringing up a new combination."

"Have you had any success?"

"I've been working on it since I was a youth," the Warden said, "and it's almost perfect. If the King will grant me a little more money, we will have a whole volume of learned writing ready very soon."

We went across the hall to another part of the Academy.

"This is our School of Languages," the Warden told me. "These men are busy improving our language."

"How do they do that?"

"Have you ever noticed how many unnecessary words there are? Look around you and what do you see? Things. That's all there are in the world. So why do we need words that don't refer to things? It's simple. Nouns are all we need. Get rid of all other words, and we could talk much faster and much more clearly. That's what these learned men used to be working on."

"But they gave up?"

"Oh, no. They went further. If words only stand for things, why do we need words at all? In order to speak, we can simply point to the thing itself. Our meaning will be completely clear. That way, we don't have to wear out our lungs speaking."

"Has the system been accepted?"

"The common people are so stubborn. They insist on speaking with their tongues as their ancestors did. But some of our most learned men have used the system and found it a wonderful way to speak."

"But what if the object isn't there to point to?"

"Well, for short conversations, these men carried things in their pockets. They could take out a knife or a turnip or a frying pan and point to it."

"That sounds simple enough."

"Of course, for longer conversations, they needed many more things. They might want to talk about a rabbit, or a razor, a fake mustache or a birdcage. They needed a whole sack of things. They would carry a candlesnuffer in case they ever needed to refer to it, and a fishing pole, a cotter pin, a thumbtack, a stepladder, and a spirit level. They needed a scythe and a spring and a scissors and a shoe. And of course, a rutabaga. Some hired two or three strong servants to carry the heavy bundles filled with all these things and more."

"That seems inconvenient."

"Yes, perhaps it was a little inconvenient. But they spoke so clearly. And the beauty was, you never needed an interpreter. If you met someone from another land, they still understood you perfectly. A pity it hasn't become more popular."

The Warden invited me to join him in the dining room.

"I just want to show you one more room before we eat. This is our Mathematics School. As you know, most students hate math. We have invented a new way to teach it."

"What method is that?"

"We write the formulas and equations on a thin sheet made from dried brain. The students eat these sheets and the brain tissue goes to their brains, taking the knowledge with it."

"How does it work?"

"So far, it hasn't worked so well. We think it may be necessary for the students to eat only bread and water for three days before swallowing the formulas. Another problem is that they often get sick to their stomachs and vomit the knowledge out before it reaches their brains. Very unfortunate. Now, are you ready for lunch?"

6

The food was very poor, as all the food was in that land.

After lunch, we toured the area of the Academy where researchers studied Political Science. There I met some of the craziest of all the members of the Academy.

These men were trying to find a way by which high government officials could be chosen by their merits and abilities. They wanted to have these officials act according to what was good for the public and to always look out for the welfare of the people.

"Do they really think these preposterous notions can ever work?" I asked the Warden. "I've never heard of anything more ludicrous."

"It's true this is one of our most difficult projects," he admitted. "But we try. One idea is to have doctors attend the sessions of the Senate. They will check the pulse of the senators and treat them for whatever seems to be bothering them."

"What kind of treatments?"

"Medicines, laxatives, headache remedies, that kind of thing."

"What else have you tried?"

"Well, when a senator makes a promise during a campaign, he often forgets it afterward. We've tried hiring servants who tweak his nose, pull his ears, or step on his foot whenever he forgets."

"Does it help?"

"I'm afraid their memories are just too poor for anything to help. Another problem is that we have political parties that can never seem to agree. We've been experimenting with a way to solve that. We operate on the leaders of each party. We remove half of each man's brain and in-sert it into the other man. We thought it would make each of them better able to run the government, but so far we haven't had much luck."

"Have any of your schemes worked?"

"We did have some success with our tax plan. Instead of taxing citizens' vices, like smoking and drinking, we taxed their virtues."

"What do you mean?"

"Well, if a man or woman claims to be a great favorite of the opposite sex, he or she has to pay a tax. If they're witty or brave or polite, each quality is taxed. Women are taxed for their beauty. We take the person's word for how great they are, then charge them."

"Not a bad idea. So you tax honor and justice and wisdom, too?"

"No, we don't bother with them. We find those qualities so rarely that it's not worth the trouble."

7

At first, I thought that Laputa and Balnibarbi were the most interesting places I had ever visited. But after touring the Academy and seeing how foolish the people were here, the whole thing became very tiresome. I just wanted to go home. But how could I do it?

I didn't know exactly where Laputa and its kingdom were located, but I knew it was in the Pacific, somewhere southeast of Japan. I hoped to make my way to Japan, where I knew I might be able to get a ship that was going back to Europe.

I learned that there was a great island to the northwest called Luggnagg. The King of Luggnagg, they said, was a great friend of the Japanese emperor. Ships traveled between the two kingdoms.

I decided to try to get to the land of Luggnagg and there try to catch a ride to Japan. I hired a guide and some mules and went over the mountains until I came to the port city of Maldonada. Unfortunately, no ship was leaving there for Luggnagg. I would have to wait for at least a month there.

A gentleman I spoke to there suggested that while I was waiting I should visit the island of Glubbdubdrib.

"It's only about fifteen miles off," he said. "I think you'll find it most interesting. I and my friend will come with you."

On the way, I asked him what Glubbdubdrib meant. He told me it was the Island of the Magicians.

"The tribe of men there are all magicians," he said. "The odd thing is, they are able to call up the dead. They can employ as servants anyone who's ever lived, but only for a day. Then they can't call them up again for three months."

We arrived at the small island about eleven in the morning. The gentleman sent word to the Governor of the island and he allowed the three of us to enter his palace.

We passed several guards, all dressed in a very crazy fashion. Something about their faces made my flesh crawl in horror.

The Governor greeted us cordially.

"I would like to hear all about your travels, Mr. Gulliver," he said. "But first let me dismiss my servants." He snapped his fingers and they all instantly disappeared.

The Governor saw that I was frightened by this and assured me that I would not be harmed. I gave him a short history of my many adventures in Lilliput, Brobdingnag and Laputa. He found my stories very interesting, but confessed that some of them were a bit hard to believe.

"You must stay for dinner," he said. We ate a very good dinner, served up by a group of ghostly servants whom he created out of thin air.

Next, the Governor said, "I've had rooms prepared for you here in the palace. Won't you stay the night?"

"That is too generous of you, Governor," I said. "But I think our plans were to sleep in town."

The others agreed. I had no desire to stay overnight in that creepy place, nor did they.

"As you like," the Governor said. He arranged for us to lodge at a private house in town.

We stayed there ten days and I got used to the ghosts, the way you get used to anything. We met frequently with the Governor and became friends.

"To entertain you," he said, "I can call up any person who ever lived. What great character from history would you like to meet?"

"How about Alexander the Great?"

He snapped his fingers. There was Alexander, dressed in his armor and looking just like a living man.

"It is said you were poisoned to death," I said in the little Greek I remembered from school. "I've always wondered if that was true."

He answered me in a form of Greek that I found hard to understand. I think he said he had not been poisoned but died of fever.

Next, the Governor called up for me, Julius Caesar and Brutus, the man who killed him. I had an interesting talk with both of them.

After that, I met with many other figures from history. I can't name them all. Sometimes I wonder if it really happened, or if I was just dreaming

8

We sailed back to the city of Maldonada and I had to wait there another two weeks before a ship left for Luggnagg. My friends, the two gentlemen I had traveled with, gave me provisions and saw me on board.

We were at sea for a month. A violent storm forced us off course and delayed our arrival. But finally on April 21, 1708, we sailed up the river of Clumegnig, on the coast of Luggnagg.

Word got out that a stranger and world traveler was on board, meaning me. The officials at the port took me to the customhouse officer, who questioned me.

"Where are you coming from and what's your business in Luggnagg?"

I gave him a short account of my travels.

"What is your nation?"

I don't know why, but I didn't want to say I was English. "Dutch," I answered. I knew that Holland was the only European country that traded with Japan.

"I was shipwrecked on the coast of Balnibarbi," I told him. "I was then taking onto the Flying Island of Laputa. I am now looking for a way to return home."

"We'll have to hold you here until we investigate you further and receive orders from the court. I'll write to them now and hope to have an answer in two weeks."

They took me to a nice house with a garden. A sentry stood guard outside, but otherwise they treated me well. Some citizens heard I had traveled to strange distant kingdoms. They came to visit me out of curiosity. I had a servant who was also my interpreter. He could speak the language of Balnibarbi, which I had learned. He translated my words into the tongue of Luggnagg.

When word came back from the capital, which is called Traldragdubb, the authorities ordered that I be brought there. A messenger was sent to the king with a request that I should have the honor to "lick the dust before his Majesty's footstool."

"Is that the way people talk at the King's court?" I asked the interpreter.

"It's not just a way of talking," he said. "You'll see that soon enough."

When I was admitted to the presence of the King I was commanded to crawl on my belly and lick the floor as I went.

"Because you're a guest here," one of the ministers said, "we've had it swept."

"You mean usually you don't sweep it?"

"No, unless the person is very important. More often, we toss more dust around. Especially if it's someone we think is an enemy of the King. Sometimes their mouths are so crammed with dirt by the time they reach the throne that they can't speak a word."

I later learned that when a man is condemned for a crime, he is ordered to lick the floor after poison has been sprinkled on it. They were careful to wash the floor afterwards. Innocent persons had died when they visited the king following such an execution and licked up some of the poison.

Anyway, I didn't like it but I crept to within a few yards of the throne, licking the floor as I went. Then I said the words they had told me to say, "May your Majesty outlive the sun by eleven moons."

The King said something back, and my interpreter said that his Majesty was delighted that I had come. He ordered his Bliffmarklub, a privileged servant, to arrange a room for me in the palace.

There I settled in and stayed for three months. While I was there, I met some of the strangest people I had encountered on all my travels.

9

While I was talking with a gentleman in the palace at Luggnagg, the man asked me if I had met any of the *Struldbruggs*.

"Are they a family here?"

"No. In our kingdom, sometimes a person is born with a red circle on his or her forehead. That means they are immortal -- they never die. There are about fifty of them living in the city right now."

"What a wonderful thing!" I cried. "How lucky that a person has a chance to be born immortal. And these wise persons must set an example for others. They must be the happiest people on earth. No worries about death. I would love to meet some of them."

He smiled at me as if he considered me ignorant or foolish. "And what would you do with yourself if you had the good fortune, as you call it, to be born immortal?"

"Well, the first thing I would do would be to get hold of plenty of money. I'd have lots of time to do it. Then I would learn all the sciences there are. Then maybe I would become a historian and record events as they happened. I would live to see the great changes that come with the ages. I would become a treasury of knowledge."

"What else?"

"I would marry a wife who was also immortal. And all my friends would be immortals. We would sit and share our wisdom all day. We would have the pleasure of seeing history unfold, kingdoms come and go, villages grow to cities, rivers dry up and become streams. We would hear about amazing discoveries and inventions."

He nodded. "Such ideas I have seen in other nations. I was ambassador to Japan once. There, the people think immortality is the greatest gift on earth. Old people always want to live one day longer. But here in Luggnagg, we have another view. Do you know why? We have learned from the Struldbruggs."

"Learned what?"

"You think that being immortal means being forever young, forever healthy. If that were so, it might be as desirable as you think. But it is not so. How would you like to be immortal if you had to live on and on with all the hardships of old age?"

"Is that how it is with the Struldbruggs?"

"They are like anyone else until they are about thirty. After that, they become sad and dejected. That mood lasts until they are eighty. Not many of us live past eighty. The Struldbuggs, at that age, are as foolish and infirm as any old people. Only worse.

"They are haunted by the prospect of never dying. They are mean and irritable, greedy and envious. They can no longer enjoy life, only suffer. When they see a funeral, they mourn. Not for the dead, for themselves. They wish they too could go to their rest. They can't. They no longer remember being young."

"I hadn't thought of that."

"You want a wife that's immortal? We don't allow two of them to marry. That would be torture, to be tied forever to another crabby, nasty old person. Their money soon runs out, so most of them are poor. They're too old to work and make more money."

"That's awful."

"It gets worse for them. At age ninety they have lost their teeth and hair. They cannot taste food or enjoy drink. They have many illnesses, but never die from them. They forget the names of objects and people. They don't have enough memory left to read books."

I told him that these people must be the unhappiest in the kingdom.

"They are. Plus, our language is like any other, always changing. After a couple hundred years, they can no longer understand the people around them. They can't hold conversations. They live like foreigners in their own country."

After telling me this, he took me to meet some of these immortals. They were young ones, only about two hundred years old. They had no interest in me or my journeys. They only wanted me to give them a *slumskudask,* a token of remembrance. By this, they meant money, but they were not allowed to beg directly.

They are hated by all the people of Luggnagg and when one of them is born, it's seen as a bad sign.

Many have asked me how these Struldbuggs looked. I can't really describe them. The youngest of them look very, very old. But as time passes, they look worse and worse.

When I next met with the King, he noted that I had met some of their Immortals.

"I would like to send a few of them back to your country with you," he said. "That would cure your people of the silly idea of wanting to live forever. They'd see what it's really like."

"Could you do that, your Majesty?" I thought perhaps it would be a good lesson for my own people.

"Unfortunately, no. The law forbids it."

10

Mr. Gulliver," the King said to me, "you're a fine fellow. You must stay here in Luggnagg. You'll find it a very pleasant place to settle down."

"I'm sure it would be, your Majesty. But I'm determined to find a way home. My wife and children are waiting for me."

"In that case, I'll give you a letter of recommendation to the Emperor of Japan. He'll see that you are taken care of. And I'll arrange for you to sail on a ship headed that way."

Before I left, he gave me 444 pieces of gold and a red diamond that I figured was worth 1,100 pounds sterling back in England.

"You are too generous, your Majesty."

"Give my best wishes to your people, Mr. Gulliver. If you ever reach home."

On May 6, 1709, I said goodbye to the King, the princes and the high officials of Luggnagg. I traveled to Glanguenstald, which is their port city. After six days, I found a ship headed for Japan. The voyage there took fifteen days, and for once we ran into no storm or disaster.

We landed in the port town of Xamoschi on the southeast coast of Japan. I showed the customs officials my letter from the King of Luggnagg, which was marked with his seal. They treated me like a very important person, giving me a carriage to use and servants to wait on me.

They sent a message to the Emperor in Tokyo.

An interpreter came to me a few days later. He knew how to speak Dutch.

"The Emperor says to treat you as a respected person," he said. "He asks, How did you come to this land?"

"I'm a merchant from Holland," I said. "I was shipwrecked in a distant land and traveled by land and sea to Luggnagg. I came here to Japan to find my countrymen and return to Europe. I ask that the Emperor do me the favor of allowing me to journey to Nagasaki."

That was the city where Dutch traders came to buy Japanese goods.

The emperor agreed to my safe passage to that port. I arrived in Nagasaki on June 9, 1709, after a long journey. I managed to find some Dutch sailors at an inn.

"What ship are you with?" I asked them.

"And who might you be?" one of them replied.

I told him my name. I had lived in Holland during my medical studies, so I spoke the language perfectly.

"I come from the province of Gelderland, way out in the country." I knew that they were unlikely to be familiar with that remote area of their nation. I made up other details, about my family and life there.

They said they were from the ship *Amboyna*, out of Amsterdam. They agreed to take me to their captain, Theodore Vangrult.

"So you want passage back to Holland, do you?" he asked.

"Yes, Captain. And I can pay my way."

"Well, my men tell me you have done duty as a ship's surgeon. It happens we are in need of one. I'll let you travel for half price if you'll take on that duty for the Amboyna."

I agreed and we soon set out for the long journey back to Europe. We rounded the Cape of Good Hope, stopping only long enough to take on water.

On April 6, 1710, we arrived in Amsterdam. Only three men died of sickness on the trip, so Captain Vangrult said I had done my job.

I soon crossed over to England. I landed in London on April 10. I had finally arrived home after five-and-a-half years. Following my journey, it felt strange to be in a place where everything was normal.

I couldn't wait to find my family and see how they were.

The End of the Third Part

Part Four

A Voyage to the
Country of the Houyhnhnms

1

I was overjoyed to discover that my wife and children were well. How the children had grown. Johnny had sprouted up and Betty was as pretty as her mother. They were amazed and delighted to see me walk in the door.

Now, finally, at long last, without question, no doubt about it, I had had my fill of traveling. If that's what you think, dear reader, you don't know me. But I think you do know me well enough to guess that I was not content to stay at home. My itch to travel was worse than ever. I had to go places or I would go mad.

So, five short months after my return, I was off to sea again. I had grown tired of being a mere ship's surgeon. I knew as much about the ways of the sea as anyone and I wanted to be in charge. As it turned out, my old ship, the *Adventure,* needed a new captain. I was hired.

So on September 7, 1710, I set out again, headed for the South Seas. On the way, several of the ship's crew died of tropical fever. We had to stop in the West Indies to hire more sailors.

Unfortunately, the men who were available there were some of the worst scoundrels I had ever met. But we needed a crew so I hired them and set sail for the Pacific. On the way, these new men turned my original crew against me. They told the other sailors how they could get rich by taking over the ship themselves.

Sure enough, one morning they rushed into my cabin and tied me up, hand and foot.

"We're taking over this ship, Captain Gulliver. And if you put up a fight, we'll throw you overboard!"

"You're an evil bunch," I said, "but you leave me with little choice but to give in."

When I promised to be their prisoner, they untied me and only fastened a chain to my leg. They gave me food and drink, but I could never leave my cabin. It reminded me of when I was a prisoner in Lilliput.

I could hear them talking on deck.

"We'll become pirates," one man said. "We'll rob other ships and get richer than any man on earth."

They all cheered at this.

"First, we have to get more men. We'll need them when we run into fights."

"Let's sell the trade goods in the hold and gather more men at Madagascar," another said.

They sailed on for many weeks, but I had no idea what course they followed or where they were going. At any moment I expected them to come in and murder me.

On May 9, 1711, one of the crewmen, James Welch, came into my cabin.

"I have orders from the captain," he told me.

"What captain?" I demanded. "I'm the captain of this ship."

He said that one of the scoundrels we had hired had named himself the new captain, but he wouldn't tell me which one.

"We're going to put you ashore, Mr. Gulliver."

"Maroon me in some unknown place?"

"It may be hard on you, sir. But to my way of thinking, it's better than being tossed overboard."

He was right, of course. He allowed me to put on my best clothes. When he wasn't looking, I slipped what money I had and some other things into my pockets. They let me keep my short sword with me as well.

They made me climb into a longboat and rowed me about three miles to land.

"What place is this?" I asked as I climbed onto the beach.

"We don't know, Mr. Gulliver," Welch said. "We are as ignorant as you. The captain said we should put you ashore at the first land we saw, and this is it. Good luck to you."

They left me there and rowed back toward the ship.

I laid down to rest for a while, feeling pretty blue and sorry that I had ever returned to sea. I decided to turn myself over to whatever savages I came across and try to win their favor with the few bracelets, glass rings and other trinkets I had brought with me.

As I made my way inland, I saw that it was a pleasant country, with lovely forests and fields of grass and oats. Perhaps the savages there were more civilized than in other wild places.

I went carefully. I didn't want to surprise the people there for fear they would shoot me with arrows before I could approach them.

Finally I came to a road where I saw the tracks of many human feet, and also those of horses.

Before I encountered any humans, I saw some strange animals in the fields. More of them were climbing trees around me. They were ugly, deformed creatures and I lay down in secret to watch them.

They had hair on their heads, backs, arms and legs, but the rest of their bodies were bare. The males wore beards like goats. They walked on all fours like apes most of the time but could stand on their hind feet when they wanted. They could climb trees as easily as a squirrel. They were very disagreeable and smelled awful. The only sounds they made were grunts and squeals.

I decided to continue on my way, hoping to come across the natives who lived in that place. But I soon found one of these awful creatures blocking my path. When he saw me, he made terrible faces, showing me his teeth. He came near and lifted his paw toward me. I drew my short sword and slapped him with the flat side of it.

He jumped back. He roared so loudly that a whole herd of these beasts came stampeding toward me. There must have been forty of them, howling and growling and baring their fangs.

I ran toward a large tree and leaned my back against it for protection. I was able to keep them off by waving my sword. But several of them leaped up the tree trunk and climbed into the branches above me. From there they tried to drop their excrement onto my head.

Eeewh! It was awful. I avoided the droppings pretty well, but the stench was terrible.

As I continued to fight for my life, I saw them all suddenly look up. They screeched to each other, then they all ran away.

I wondered what was frightening them. I turned and saw a horse walking out of the field. Was this what had scared them? The horse seemed surprised to see me, but stared at me with curiosity.

I started to go on my way, but this horse now stood in my path and seemed to be studying me. He seemed very tame, so I reached out to pat his neck, giving him a little whistle the way jockey's do.

He disliked my touching him and gently pushed my hand away with his hoof. He neighed three or four times, but with a noise I had never heard a horse make, as if he were speaking a language of his own.

At that point, another horse appeared. The two of them neighed to each other. Then they went off a little way and seem to be talking together. I was amazed to see such behavior in dumb beasts. I figured the people who lived in this country must be pretty smart if they trained their horses so well.

I began to sneak off, hoping to find a house or village where I could meet some of the natives. The first horse, a dapple gray, made a sound that somehow called me back. The way he looked at me made me nervous. I came near him, trying to hide my fear.

Now both horses looked me over very carefully. They seemed especially interested in my clothing, which they touched with their hooves. And they examined my hands and face, testing the softness of the skin.

An idea occurred to me.

"I know exactly what you are," I said at last. "You're magicians who have taken on the form of horses. If that's true, maybe you can understand any language, including English."

The horses looked at each other and made whinnying sounds.

"I want you to know I'm an English sea captain who's been abandoned on your shores. I hope that one of you will allow me to ride on his back to the nearest town. I'll repay you with this knife and bracelet." I took the items out of my pocket.

They listened very patiently, but did not understand. They began to neigh to each other and I was able to see that this was definitely a language they were speaking. I heard them repeat the word *Yahoo* a number of times.

So I said *Yahoo* myself, imitating the neighing of a horse. The two horses were very surprised. They repeated the word as if to correct my accent. I said it again correctly.

The second horse taught me another word, harder to pronounce. I can only write it as *Houyhnhnm*. I repeated this, not knowing what it meant. They were both amazed.

The gray horse made a sign that I should walk with them. I did not dare defy them.

Every time I slowed down, one of the horses would cry, *Hhuun! Hhuun!* I guess they meant hurry up, but I made a sign that I was tired, so they let me rest.

I had no idea where they were taking me or what kind of weird world I found myself in this time.

2

We walked about three miles through the countryside. Finally, we came to a low, shed-like building made of posts stuck into the ground and a thatched roof. They must have brought me to the home of the natives who live in this land, I thought. I searched my pockets for some trinkets to give them so they would treat me kindly.

But there was no one inside the shed, only three older horses and two mares. They weren't eating, as you would expect in a stable, but sitting down. It seemed very strange. When I came in, several of them jumped up and seemed as if they would attack me, but the gray horse neighed to them several times and they stopped.

The gray horse led me through to another room and motioned for me to wait while he entered a third. This, I thought, must be where the master of the house lives. I took out my gifts again -- some bracelets, small knives, and a bead necklace. I heard the horse neigh, but I waited until the humans invited me inside.

Yet while I stood there, I heard no human voices, only the gray horse and some other horses whinnying in low tones. Could all of these people's servants be horses? That would be very odd.

Again I suspected that these were all magicians or sorcerers. Perhaps they had put a spell on me. I pinched myself to try to wake up.

The gray horse came to the door and made a motion that I should enter the last room. There I saw a very nice looking mare with a colt and a foal. They were sitting on their haunches on clean straw mats.

The mare rose and came near me. She gave me a dirty look and seemed to speak to the gray horse. I heard the word *Yahoo* repeated several times by both of them. What could it mean?

Then the gray horse led me out of the shed, repeating, *Hhuun, Hhu-un,* to urge me along. We went out into a courtyard and entered a different building. There I saw three of those awful creatures I had first met on coming ashore. Each was tied by the neck to a post, just like a dog. They were eating raw meat, which they held with the claws of their forefeet and tore at with their teeth.

The big gray ordered a sorrel horse to untie one of the creatures and lead him into the yard. There, the two horses looked carefully at the creature and at me. Several times they said, Yahoo.

I now realized that *Yahoo* meant this type of beast. This was a Yahoo.

Now I looked at the creature more carefully myself. As I studied him, a horror came over me. I saw that he had the form of a human! His face was flat, his nails were long like claws, he was remarkably hairy. But his hands, his eyes, his feet, in all these he was just like me.

Of course, the horses could not see the entire resemblance because I was wearing clothes and this creature was naked. They seemed puzzled by both my likeness to this Yahoo and the ways that I was different.

The sorrel horse offered me a piece of raw meat. It smelled so bad that I turned away in disgust. He tossed it to the creature beside me, who grabbed it and gnawed on it eagerly.

The horse then offered me a bit of hay. I shook my head to indicate that this was not my kind of food, either.

I saw that I must starve if I did not find some real humans in this land. I could not believe that these awful, ugly creatures were the only human-like here. I couldn't stand being near them.

The gray horse seemed to sense this. He sent the Yahoo back and made a motion to know what I would eat. Luckily, I saw a cow passing. I signaled to him that I wished to milk her. He had his servant horse take me to a room where there was a good store of milk in clean earthen containers. He gave me a large bowl of it. I drank it down and found it very refreshing.

About noon a kind of sled appeared drawn by four Yahoos. On it was an older horse, who appeared to be a noble among them. He was treated with respect by the other horses. They sat down to dinner and talked among themselves. The older horse kept looking at me and repeating *Yahoo.*

The gray horse saw that I had put on my gloves. He motioned as if to say, "What has happened to your forefeet?"

I removed the gloves and all the horses were quite surprised.

Now he taught me the names for oats, milk, fire, water and some other words. I asked for oats, which they call *hlunnh*. I had to eat something.

I heated these oats by the fire and rubbed the husks off. Then I ground them between two stones, added water to make cakes, and toasted those by the fire. They tasted very bland, but I was hungry and had to eat. And they must have been good for me, because I was never sick while I stayed on this island.

As night came on, the gray horse showed me a place I could sleep. Fortunately, it was not too close to where they kept the Yahoos. I covered myself with straw and slept soundly.

The next day I set out to learn the language of that land, so that I could talk with these amazing creatures.

3

All the horses thought I was something quite wonderful, a brute animal who could actually speak their language. I kept pointing to things and they would tell me the names. I wrote them all down in my notebook.

At first, I spoke with a bad accent, but I kept asking to hear the words again and tried to repeat them as closely as I could. They use mostly their nose and throat to pronounce a word, as you would expect a horse to.

I wrote the words as best I could using English letters. These creatures had no writing and no books.

My master, the gray horse, spent hours every day teaching me. He was convinced I must be a kind of Yahoo. To him, that made me very curious. I was certainly the smartest Yahoo any of them had ever heard of.

They didn't know what to make of my clothes. Some thought they were part of my body, some didn't. I wasn't about to explain. I never undressed until all the horses were asleep, and I was always sure to put my clothes back on before they woke. I was ashamed of how much I looked like a Yahoo.

After three months, I could speak quite well.

"Explain," my master asked me, "why you are so much like a Yahoo. Yet those are the stupidest, most unteachable creatures in the world and you seem a very quick learner."

"I come from a distant land where all the people are more or less like me," I told him. "I traveled here in a hollow vessel made from the bodies of trees, but my companions forced me to come ashore on this coast."

"You must be mistaken," he said. "You have said the thing which is not."

I realized that they had no word for lie or falsehood. This phrase, *the thing which is not,* was as close as they could come.

"There are no countries beyond the sea," he went on, "And there could be none ruled by brutes like the Yahoos. Therefore, you must have said the thing which is not."

He told me that the word Houyhnhnm in their language means not only "horse" but "perfection of nature." This, he said, was the land of the Houyhnhnms. He was a Houyhnhnm.

Other horses now arrived quite regularly to see the Yahoo-like creature who could speak like a Houyhnhnm. I was considered quite a sensation.

"He even seems to have a primitive sense of reason," one of them said.

"Could he really be a Yahoo?" another asked.

"I doubt it," said a third. "Where's his hair? Why is his body so different from those of the vile Yahoos?"

In order to sleep better, I was in the habit of taking off my clothes and using them as a kind of blanket. One night, the sorrel horse came to deliver a message from my master. He saw that my clothes had fallen to the side. There I was, stark naked.

He ran back to his master, all in a fright, and reported what he had seen. Soon I was called in to speak with the gray horse.

"You are a different creature when you sleep than you are when you are awake," he said. "How do you explain this?"

I saw that there was no use trying to hide the truth any longer. Some day my clothes would wear out and I would need new ones. I had to be truthful. Anyway, I was growing to dislike any form of falsehood or secrecy.

"In the land I come from, everyone covers his or her body with the hair of certain animals woven into cloth," I said. "We do it to keep off the harsh weather and also because nature teaches us to hide certain parts of our bodies."

"Why would nature want to hide what nature has made?" he asked.

"I can't explain that, but I can show you what I really look like. You should be prepared for a shock."

I removed my coat and vest, my shoes, socks and pants. I stood there in only my underwear. My master watched with great curiosity. He looked over my clothes, touching them with his hoof.

"So it's true. Except for the whiteness and smoothness of your skin, you are indeed a perfect Yahoo," he said. "Yes, you have very short claws and you always walk on your hind feet. But there's no question. You're one of them."

"I beg you not to call me that," I said. "I admit that I look like the Yahoos. But I have nothing but hatred for those awful creatures. I am not a wild beast."

I also asked him not to reveal my secret to the other horses. I was afraid they would think me nothing but a Yahoo and turn against me.

He agreed not to discuss my true nature with the others.

We again talked about how I had reached the land of the Houyhnhnms.

"Who made this marvelous vessel that you use to sail over the ocean?"

"Men like myself," I said.

"But how could the Houyhnhnms of your land leave something like that to mere brutes?"

"I don't want to offend you, Master, but in my land we would be as surprised to find reason in a Houyhnhnm as you are to find reason in a creature like me, who looks so much like a Yahoo."

"I hope you are not saying the thing which is not," he replied. "Your story is quite astounding. But tell me more."

My master explained to me why "saying the thing which is not" was considered such a terrible thing among them.

"The purpose of speaking is to understand each other, is it not?" he asked.

"Yes, of course."

"If you say the thing which is not, it's worse than not understanding. If you say a thing is black when it's really white, or short when it's really long, I am worse than ignorant. I believe what is not."

"Nevertheless," I had to admit, "in my land, it's very common to say the thing which is not. People do it every day."

"That I don't understand."

I tried to explain, but I found it hard to think of all the reasons that humans tell lies and fibs to each other.

"And are there really Houyhnhnms in this land you come from?"

"Oh yes. Some of them are kept in pastures in the summer and in warm barns with hay and oats in the winter. Humans take care of them and brush them and make their beds."

"I wish our Yahoos attended us as well," he said. "So the Houyhnhnms are your masters?"

"I'm afraid if I tell you the truth, you will be very unhappy," I said.

"No, I want to know everything, as long as it's true."

"Many Houyhnhnms, as I have said, are treated kindly and generously. But most are kept by farmers and carriers. They make them work very hard plowing and pulling wagons. I'm afraid they treat them quite badly. They use a bit and bridle to ride them. They harness them and drive them with a whip and spurs. They nail iron shoes to their hooves so they can work harder."

I had to explain to him what these words meant. He frowned deeply when I described a whip and how it was used.

He was shocked to hear all of this.

"How do you dare climb on the back of a Houyhnhnm? What right do you have? Why do the Houyhnhnms put up with it? They could easily roll over and knock one of you weak creatures off."

"They have no choice. They are trained from the age of two that if they don't, they will be punished. You see, in our country the Houyhnhnms have no more reason than the Yahoos have here."

"That's absurd!" he said. "To think that Houyhnhnms could be treated so."

He asked me what the creatures who ruled my land were like. "Are they like you, or like the Yahoos here?"

"They are much more like me. They are clean and not so deformed or savage as the Yahoos."

"But you're worse than a Yahoo. You have no claws. Your feet are too soft to walk around without coverings. You traipse about so much on your hind feet that you could easily fall. You can't stand the heat or cold. You're much weaker than any Yahoo."

"Nevertheless, Master," I said, "what I'm telling you is true."

"You say that creatures like you are in charge of the land you come from. You say it's because of your superior reason. Yet you tell me that you are always fighting among yourselves. You have this thing called war. How do you explain that?"

"Give me a moment and I will try to clear it up for you."

5

It's true," I explained, "that the creatures in my land often go to war. But they have very good reasons. Sometimes, their leaders are ambitious. They want to control more land and people. Sometimes the people in two lands disagree about religion. They have to decide the matter by fighting. Or they may not like the way the people in another country look. So they go to war. Or they want the things that others have, so they fight to take them. Or they want to civilize another group of people. Or make them slaves. Or they are allies with another country which has quarrel with a third nation. So you see, there all sorts of good reasons to go to war."

"And your creatures don't see the foolishness of all of these reasons?"

"No, we consider a warrior to be a very honorable profession. And of course, whichever warrior can kill the greatest number of his own species is the most honored of all."

He was still puzzled. "You describe these wars and say that many thousands are killed. But if these creatures are like you, with dull teeth and no claws to speak of, how can they kill?"

I shook my head and smiled at his ignorance.

"We have guns and cannons, swords and bayonets. We throw bombs at each other." I tried to explain what these words meant, but he had trouble understanding.

"So that's how you act when you in a war?" he asked.

"Yes. And we charge each other riding on Houyhnhnms. Why, I have seen our best warriors blow up a hundred men at a time. I have seen them sink ships, killing five hundred."

"Your description makes me hate the whole species. I thought the Yahoos were bad. But they have not a spark of reason. They are no more cruel than a *gnnayh*." He meant by this a common bird of prey there. "But for a creature who can reason to carry on the way you describe, that's awful. There's no excuse for it."

"I can assure you, Master, that if you saw things the way we see them, you would understand."

"I doubt it. But I want to ask you about another odd thing you mentioned. This thing you call *money*."

6

"Money," I explained, "is made out of a metal that is very precious to us. When a Yahoo in my land has a store of it, he can go out and buy whatever he wants -- the best clothes, a grand house, land, and wonderful food. As a result, the Yahoos there never can have enough of it."

Yes, I had begun to speak of my fellow men as Yahoos. And to see them as very low and mean creatures.

"And what do they do with it?" my master asked.

"Some love to spend it. Others love to save it. All think of nothing but trying to get more."

"But how do they get it?"

"The rich men make money from the labor of the poor ones. Most, of course, have very little money and have to work hard just to get by."

"But don't all animals have a right to a share of the products of the earth?"

"I don't know about that. All I know is that it takes a lot of money to gather goods from all over the world that our Yahoos want. They send ships to China for spices, for example. They send them to the Indies for tobacco and to Italy for wine. All of that costs money."

"That must be a miserable country," he said, "to have to send around the world just for things to eat and drink. Is there no fresh water? Why do you have to bring bottles of drink from far away?"

"Water, yes. We have plenty of that. But what we like to drink is wine."

"What is wine?"

"It's a liquid we swallow that makes us merry. It gives us wild ideas and raises our hopes and gets rid of our fears. Of course, it also leaves us feeling sick and miserable. And in the long run, it can make a person very ill."

"You say that your job back in your land is to care for those Yahoos who become ill," he said. "What does this mean? We Houyhnhnms do grow weak a few days before we die. But we do not know this illness. It seems impossible to me that, as you say, those in your country should suffer so much illness."

"Perhaps," I said, "it's because we drink strong liquors. We eat when we are not hungry. We stay up nights. We don't look after ourselves."

"I think you're right. We say in our country that too much is always bad. Too much salt, juice, seaweed, bark, bones, fish, whatever it is."

I said that in our country, in addition to real diseases, we suffered from many imaginary illnesses.

"What do you do for those?"

"Our doctors have invented imaginary cures."

He shook his head at the foolishness of my people.

But I observed that his fellows were not completely without prejudice. They thought that the white, sorrel and iron-gray horses were not so beautiful as the bay, dapple-gray and black. As a result, the white, sorrel and iron-gray were almost always servants, while the others ran things. I honestly couldn't tell the difference, other than their color.

7

As months, then years, passed, I had many talks with my master. My opinion of humans sank lower and lower. I could not defend all their bad habits and stupidity. Like the Houyhnhnms, I developed a hatred of falsehood. I never wanted to say the thing which was not.

The more I thought about it, the more I lost all desire to return to my home or to live among humans. I wanted to spend the rest of my life among the good Houyhnhnms. By following their example, I would lead a life of peaceful goodness.

One morning, my master called me to him.

"Sit down, Lemuel," he said. It was an honor. He had never allowed me to sit in his presence before. "I have listened to you talk many times about these creatures who are your people. I grant that you may have a small bit of reason, not much. But you seem to use it only to make yourselves worse. You spend your whole lives trying to satisfy wants that you make up yourselves. You are like Yahoos, but you have neither the strength nor the speed nor the ability to climb trees that your brothers have."

I hated for him to call those beasts my brothers. But I held my tongue.

"You come from a country where reason is used to distort government, to misrule, to cause cruelties. Your people are always eager, as you yourself admit, to say the thing which is not."

I tried to think of something to say in the defense of humans, but I could not.

"You are different than Yahoos, but I think you are also very much like them. For example, if you take enough food to feed fifty Yahoos and throw it to only five, they will still fight over it. I've seen it happen. In fact, I've seen the Yahoos fight for no reason at all."

"I know this is true. I've seen it here myself."

"There are in our country certain shining stones of different colors," he said. "If the Yahoos find them, they will dig them out of the ground with their claws. All day they'll work to get at them. They'll pile them near their caves and look around suspiciously. The stones are of no use to them, but they're afraid some other Yahoo will come and take them. And if that happens, you should hear them cry and carry on."

I could not help seeing the resemblance of this behavior to that of humans. The Yahoos treated the stones the way humans treated money.

"And Yahoos, if they find food, will eat and eat and eat until they're ready to burst. Of all the animals here, they're the only ones to suffer from disease. They're the only ones who go around dirty. All other animals clean themselves."

The more he talked about Yahoos, the more I grew to hate them. Even so, I had a strange desire to go among them and learn more about them. I thought by doing so, I could understand humans better.

I asked my master for permission to do so. He said I could, but that I should take the sorrel horse with me to guard me. I agreed.

8

We had not gone far before we saw a herd of Yahoos in the distance. When we drew near, they showed their hatred of me, imitating me the way monkeys do.

I had long observed that these Yahoos can learn nothing. The only tasks they do well are things like drawing sleds or carrying burdens for the Houyhnhnms. They are strong, but cowardly and cruel.

They eat roots and plants and whatever meat they can find. They kill weasels and *luhimuhs*, which us a kind of wild rat. They sleep in holes they dig with their claws.

They can swim very well and often catch fish. I learned about that the very day we went out Yahoo watching.

It happened to be very hot. After studying the Yahoos for some hours, I told the sorrel horse I planned to take a swim in a nearby stream. No sooner was I in the water than a female Yahoo leaped into the water and swam toward me. I couldn't move fast enough to get away.

She grabbed me. I don't know if she had fallen in love with me or wanted to harm me. Anyway, she was very strong and in another minute she would have drowned me.

I managed to get off a shout. The sorrel horse came galloping over. He splashed into the water and forced her to let me go.

She climbed onto the far bank as I dragged myself out of the water. She stood there howling her head off and making frightening gestures.

My Master and his family laughed at this when they heard about it. It sure wasn't funny to me.

I had had enough of Yahoos. They looked even worse to me in relation to my hosts, the Houyhnhnms.

All the horses there were friendly toward each other. When a stranger came from a distant part of the island, he was made to feel at home. They brought up their young right, educating them and treating them kindly. They did not show preference for their own colts and foals, but treated all with love.

They made sure that the young had time to graze in the fields, and to get exercise. They taught them cleanliness and industry. They thought that humans were monsters to educate males but not females, as if women were good for nothing but bringing children into the world.

The young Houyhnhnms ran up and down steep hills to develop their strength. They practiced leaping and swimming. Four times a year, the youth of different districts met to test their skills against each other. The winner was rewarded by having a song made up in his or her honor. Then they had a feast of oats and hay.

Every four years, on the first day of spring, a council of the Houyhnhnm met on a plain to discuss any issues that needed to be taken care of. I had the privilege to attend one of these meetings. A great question was to be decided and I was surprised when I found out what it was. I was even more shocked at what came next.

I'll tell you about it in the next chapter.

9

My master told me I could observe the assembly if I hid in the bushes at the edge of the plain and kept quiet. I watched as horses from all over the island gathered together.

"The issue to be decided," said the horse who seemed to be one of the leaders, "is whether all the Yahoos should be killed."

There were shouts from many in support of this idea.

"They are the dirtiest, most foul and deformed animals in this land," one horse said. "You can't teach them a thing. They're always getting into some mischief. They steal milk from our cows, eat our cats, trample the oats, and do many other nasty things. I say we should exterminate them once and for all."

"I agree," said another. "Remember, they haven't always been here. It's said that the heat of the sun on the mud and slime is what bred them. These Yahoos, which came from the ooze, soon were running all around our land."

"But Yahoos are useful," a black horse stated. "We all know that. Once they're tamed, they carry loads and pull sleds. How could we get along without them?"

"By using donkeys, the way our grandfathers did," said another. "Donkeys are just as hard workers as Yahoos and don't have the foul smell."

"Donkeys eat too much of our own hay and oats," said the black one. "And they bray something awful."

"The Yahoos' howling is worse."

"I have a theory." It was my master speaking. "You all know that I have a certain wonderful Yahoo at home who can reason and speak. He came from across the sea. I think that our Yahoos came to this land in the same way. A few of them landed here centuries ago and took to the hills. Over time, they declined into the beasts that we know today."

"This is an interesting idea," said the leader, "but what should we do with them, that's the question."

"I say killing them all is too drastic," said my master. "We should begin to breed more donkeys. Later, when they're ready, we can begin to reduce the number of Yahoos."

They talked about it some more. Most of the horses agreed with my master. They decided on some ways to increase the population of donkeys and to feed them.

"There's one other issue we need to discuss," said the lead horse. He turned toward my master. "That's this Yahoo that you're keeping in your house. The one you think is so wonderful."

"It's not right," said another horse. "To have a Yahoo living with your family? To talk with him? It's disgusting. We all think so."

They all sounded their agreement.

"You have two choices," the leader told my master. "You can put your Yahoo to work, like any ordinary Yahoo. Or you can make him swim back to whatever place he came from."

"Is this your suggestion?" my Master asked.

"It is," said the leader. All the others agreed. Among the Houyhnhnms, no one can be ordered to do anything. But when the Assembly suggests something, the person whom they are addressing usually goes along.

The whole thing made my blood run cold. Of course, I couldn't swim back home. And anyway, the last thing in the world I wanted was to return to live among humans. Or, as I thought of them, Yahoos.

10

As time passed, I had grown very comfortable in the land of the Houyhnhnms. I was able to grow hemp and, with the fibers, make a mattress cover. I filled this with feathers from birds that I trapped. Using my knife, I had managed to put together two chairs.

When my original clothes wore out, I made new ones from rabbit skins and the skins of *nnuhnohs*, which were beautiful animals about the same size as a rabbit. I made soles for my shoes out of wood. When the uppers wore out, I replaced them, using the skins of Yahoos, which are quite tough when tanned.

I found wild honey in trees and ate it with my bread.

No one could have been happier than I was. I enjoyed perfect health and slept soundly every night. I didn't need to bribe anyone, or flatter anyone, or beg favors of anyone. I had no secret enemies. I didn't need to put up a fence or use a lock to secure my home. There were no doctors to ruin my health or lawyers to take my wealth.

But didn't you miss your fellow men? you might ask. Didn't you feel the need for the company of your own kind?

Did I miss pickpockets? Miss robbers and housebreakers? Gamblers? Bullies and drunkards? Did I feel the need of the company of politicians? Tedious bores? Murderers? No, not at all.

It didn't bother me that there were no prisons there, no courts. No pride or vanity. No stupid, boasting idiots. No quarrelsome people. No noblemen pretending to be superior to everyone else.

The talks I had with the Houyhnhnms were always educational. I learned new things every day about virtue and goodness. When they talk together, there are no interruptions or heated differences of opinion. A short silence, they think, improves conversation.

They talked about friendship and helping others. About the right use of reason. About topics that were likely to come up in the next Assembly. And often they discussed poetry, of which they were masters.

Sometimes they talked about mankind. Many visitors were anxious to find out what my Master had learned about the strange land where Yahoos ruled. What he said was not very favorable to us humans. He was able to list all our vices and weaknesses, including some I had never mentioned. He must have learned of them by studying the Yahoos in his country.

All the time, I observed how intelligent, how strong and beautiful the Houyhnhnms were. I learned to love and respect them.

When I remembered those people I knew in England, I now thought of them as what they were, Yahoos. Even my friends and relatives. They spoke better than the Yahoos here and had certain refinements, yes. But, all things considered, they were the same.

Whenever I saw my own image reflected in the water of a lake, I turned away in horror. I too was one of them, little better than a common Yahoo. The idea disgusted me.

Over time, I had begun to imitate the way Houyhnhnms walked and gestured. I would trot like a horse when I went somewhere. My voice began to sound like theirs. The more I became like them, the prouder I was of myself.

I was set for life. That is, I was until that day when I heard the Assembly suggest to my Master that he get rid of me.

How could I return to live among Yahoos? The idea filled me with grief. Under the influence of those vile creatures, I would become like them myself. I would begin to cheat and scheme and say the thing which is not. I began sometimes to wish I was dead so that I would never have to go back.

My master, as always, was kind to me.

"I cannot act against the wishes of the Assembly, Lemuel," he told me. "And I will never put you to work like an ordinary Yahoo. So you will have to try to make your way home."

"But Master, I cannot possibly swim more than a mile or so."

"I understand. I will have my servants help you build a vessel like the one you came in. You will have two months to get ready."

"Thank you, Master. If I ever make it home, I will spend my days praising the Houyhnhnms and teaching about their many virtues. The Yahoos there must know about your way of life. Maybe they can use their reason and learn from you, as I have."

"Perhaps," he said. "I doubt it, though."

Sadly, I too doubted it.

With the help of the sorrel horse, I cut some oak saplings and made the frame of a large canoe. This I covered with the skins of Yahoos, stitching them together with hemp thread that I made. I made sails of these same animals' hides. I carved four paddles.

I tried out the canoe in a large pond. I found that I needed to fill all the gaps with tallow cooked from Yahoo fat. Soon I had made it quite seaworthy.

Next, I gathered a store of boiled rabbit meat, jugs of water and others of milk.

When the time came for me to depart, tears came to my eyes.

"Good bye, Master," I said to the gray horse.

I got down onto my knees to kiss his hoof. But instead, he did me the great honor of raising it to my lips. I know many people will be shocked to hear about this. They will not be able to believe that such a fine and noble creature would show such kindness to some low wretch like me. I can only say that it is yet another sign that Houyhnhnms are among the most courteous and generous beings on earth.

The tide came in. The wind was up. So off I went. I can't tell you how sorry I was to leave that wonderful place.

11

It was nine in the morning on February 15, 1715, when I began my voyage away from the land of the Houyhnhnms. I paddled until I got out into the open ocean, then set my sails.

I looked back and saw my master and his friends watching me from the shore. I heard the sorrel horse, who had become a great friend of mine, crying out, *Hnuy illa nyha maiah Yahoo!* That means, Take care of yourself, gentle Yahoo!

My plan was to discover some island where there were no people but enough food and drink to keep me alive. There I would spend the rest of my life. I did not like the idea, but it would be a better fate by far than to return to a society ruled by Yahoos.

Remember that, when the crew of my ship rebelled some five years earlier, they kept me locked in my cabin for weeks. I had no idea where I was. Somewhere in the Indian Ocean, I assumed. Maybe south of the Cape of Good Hope.

I decided to sail eastward, hoping to reach an island somewhere off the coast of New Holland. I had a good wind and sailed all day. I was anxious to reach land, for I knew that my canoe would not be able to stand up to a storm if one came.

Finally I spied a small island in the distance. When I reached it, I found that it was nothing but rock, with one small creek. I certainly could not live there.

I climbed to the highest point and looked through my telescope. I saw a coast far off in the distance. So I climbed back into my canoe and sailed all night. I arrived at the southeastern tip of New Holland in the morning.

I saw no one living near the place where I landed. I had no weapon, so I was afraid of exploring inland. I might be surprised by the natives.

I found some clams and oysters and ate them raw. I didn't dare start a fire to cook for fear of giving myself away.

For three days I lived like this, eating what I could find to save the provisions I had brought with me. Fortunately, there was a brook nearby with excellent drinking water.

On the fourth day, I decided to explore a little way. I made my way inland. Sure enough, I came across a group of thirty natives sitting around a fire. Unfortunately, they saw me at the same time I saw them. Five of them started coming toward me.

I ran as fast as I could back toward the shore. They saw me run and chased after me. I managed to reach my canoe and shoved off into the water.

But I wasn't able to get away fast enough. One of the savages fired an arrow that hit me in the left knee (I still have the scar to this day).

I paddled as hard as I could until I was out of range of their arrows. Because I was afraid the arrow might be poisoned, I sucked on the wound and applied a bandage made from some hemp cloth I had brought with me.

What shall I do now? I asked myself. I didn't dare go back, but the wind was against me. I was trying to decide what to do when I saw a sail in the distance. A ship!

At first I was relieved. Then I remembered that any ship would be manned by Yahoos. I hated them so much, I thought I would rather take my chances with the natives of that wild place.

So I sailed back the way I had come and landed near the same creek that I had left a few hours earlier. I paddled up it and pulled my canoe out and hid behind a rock.

The ship stopped about a mile from the creek. I could see them putting down their longboat and rowing toward shore. I realized it wasn't because they had seen me, it was to get fresh drinking water from this stream.

When the sailors landed, they spotted my canoe. They looked it over and decided that the owner must be near. Four of them, armed with muskets, began looking. They soon found me, flat on my face behind the stone.

"Will you look at this," one of the seamen said in Portuguese, which I understood well.

"What is it?" another said.

"An odd character wearing strange clothing made from some kind of skins and wooden shoes. Looks like a scarecrow. Get up there, you!"

"He's not a native of this place, I can see that," his companion said.

"Who are you?"

I said, "I'm a poor Yahoo. I have been banished from the land of the Houyhnhnms. Please let me go. I will do you no harm."

They all fell to laughing when they heard the strange way I spoke, more like a horse than a man.

"He must be a European," the first sailor said. "But what's this about Yahoos and Houyhnhnms?"

"I'll be going now," I said.

One of them grabbed my arm as I stepped toward my canoe. "Just a minute there, Mister. What country are you from?"

"England," I said. "When I left my home five years ago, we were at peace with Portugal. I hope you won't treat me as an enemy. I mean no harm. I'm a poor Yahoo and only want to live out my life in some deserted place."

They talked among themselves. It shocked me to hear such creatures making intelligent sounds. In the land I had left, Yahoos never spoke.

"You certainly are an odd one," the first sailor said. "But we are not barbarians. Maybe our captain will carry you back to Lisbon. From there, you could get a ship to England."

"I wish to do nothing of the kind."

"We'll see about that."

He ordered a group of sailors to row out to the ship, tell the captain what they had found, ask him for his orders.

"And you," he said to me, "must give your word you won't run away. Otherwise, we'll have to tie you up."

I gave my word.

When the men came back, they said the captain wanted me brought aboard. I fell onto my knees and begged them to let me go. They wouldn't.

Soon I found myself in the captain's cabin. His name was Pedro de

Mendez, a pleasant, generous person. He asked me what I wanted to eat or drink.

I was surprised to find a Yahoo acting so courteously. I could hardly answer, though. I found the smell of him and his men repulsive. And I could barely bring myself to look at their deformed faces.

"I only want to be set free and returned to my canoe," I said.

"Nonsense." He ordered a meal of chicken and excellent wine. Afterward, he showed me to a clean cabin with a bed.

I didn't sleep though. I waited until I figured they were at dinner, then snuck out and prepared to jump overboard. I would do anything not to be taken back the land of the Yahoos.

But one of the seamen saw me and I soon found myself chained in my cabin.

"Why did you try to escape?" Don Pedro asked me after dinner. "We have treated you with nothing but kindness."

I gave him a short account of how I had been the captain of a ship myself, how my crew had mutinied, and how I had found myself in the land of the Houyhnhnms.

But he could not believe me. "I'm afraid this is all in your imagination," he said.

I was greatly offended. I had completely lost the habit of saying the thing which is not. How dare he accuse me of a falsehood?

"In the land of the Houyhnhnms, not even the lowest servant would ever tell a lie," I said. "But you Yahoos take it for granted. That's your nature."

"You mistake me," the captain said. "In fact, I now remember once speaking with a Dutch captain who told a story of landing on an island to the south of here. He saw horses driving before them creatures like the ones you describe. At the time I thought he was just making it up."

He wanted me to give my word of honor that I would not try to escape the ship again before he would let me loose.

"I do it, but I don't want to," I said. "Any life would be better than to return to England."

He offered to bring me one of his spare suits of clothes. I couldn't accept it. I didn't want to put on anything that had touched a Yahoo's body. I accepted only a couple of clean shirts. I made sure they had been washed several times before wearing them, but they still smelled of Yahoo.

When we arrived in Lisbon, Don Pedro took me to his own home.

"Don't speak of the things you told me about," he said. "Those stories will make people here curious about you and may even get you arrested as a crackpot."

He had a new suit made for me and treated me with all hospitality. I even began to like him, as much as I could like any Yahoo.

At first, I was afraid to go into the street among so many other Yahoos. When I finally did so, I had to stop up my nose with tobacco, so great was the stench of those creatures.

"I know you don't want to return home," Don Pedro said to me after I had stayed with him ten days. "But you owe it to your family. There's an English ship leaving soon. I will pay your passage."

"I would rather find a deserted island to live on," I said.

"You'll never do so. But if you go home, you can live in your own house and not see anyone, if that's what you want."

His argument made sense and I agreed to go. I left Lisbon on November 24, 1715. Pedro lent me some money and saw me aboard an English cargo ship.

I stayed in my cabin, pretending I was sick. During the whole voyage, I never spoke to the crew or captain. On December 5 we reached England.

As you can imagine, my wife and children were very surprised to see me.

"We thought you were dead, dear Lemuel," Mary said. "Now our prayers are answered. You're home at last!"

She took me into her arms and kissed me over and over. The touch of a Yahoo was so distressing to me that I fainted.

"Don't come near me," I said when I came to. I could not bear to be close to any Yahoo, even my own family members.

They were puzzled, but they obeyed my wishes. They probably thought that the stress of the journey had made me slightly crazy.

I had to give them strict instructions. They were to keep their distance. They shouldn't take my hand. They must never touch my food or eat in the same room with me.

I went out and bought two fine young horses and built them a good stable. My neighbors probably think it odd that I never ride them or use them to draw a carriage. I spend much of my time with them. I talk with them about four hours a day and they seem to understand me quite well.

12

So that's the story of my travels. I have left out many strange things that happened, for fear that you would not believe me. Everything I have told you is true. For, as you know, after living with the Houyhnhnms, I could never again say the thing which is not .

I remember reading all those travel books when I was a boy. Now that I have journeyed to many places myself, I know that much of what they contain is not true. I wish they would pass a law against publishing such falsehoods and tall tales.

Now, it may be that travelers who visit the lands that I mention in this book will find that things are different in those places than what I describe. If that's so, it's only because I have made honest mistakes. I am not writing to gain fame, but only to instruct my readers and promote the public good.

Some have said that it was my duty as a traveler to claim the lands I discovered for the Crown. I disagree. The tiny Lilliputians are hardly worth sending an army and fleet to conquer. And I'm afraid it wouldn't be a good idea for our armies to try to defeat the Brobdingnagians. Our forces could easily be squashed. Even the inhabitants of the Flying Island would be a dangerous enemy.

As for the Houyhnhnms, I think it would be better if they conquered us. Then they could teach us all about truth, justice, public spirit, friendship and generosity. We have words for all these things, but we really don't understand the ideas at all.

Anyway, I don't think that establishing colonies around the world is a noble work. What are we but pirates, ravaging the lands of the natives and killing them?

Nor do those people have any desire of the great benefits we say we bring them. For some reason, they do not like being enslaved or murdered so that we can steal their gold, silver, sugar and tobacco.

These days, I live my life in my own house and garden in London. I have been trying to teach my family the valuable lessons I learned from the Houyhnhnms. In time, I may be able to tolerate the presence and sight of human creatures. Now, I still find them to resemble Yahoos too closely. I can't even look at myself in a mirror. I don't want to be reminded of what I am.

I cannot bear to think of the brutality that is the fate of the Houyhnhnms in my own land. How much better it would be to treat horses with respect and kindness.

Last week, I began to allow my wife to sit at dinner with me. We talk together a little. I have lost all fear that she will attack me with her teeth and claws.

I have resigned myself to most of the vices that Yahoos practice. I can see a pickpocket or a gambler, a liar or a thief, and not be too upset. I can even tolerate traitors and lawyers and politicians and fools.

But there's one vice, very common among Yahoos, that I find absolutely intolerable. What is it? Pride.

That's right, pride. The idea that we deformed, corrupt creatures, so given to all vices and all foolishness, could take pride in ourselves—it's simply unbelievable.

Think of the noble Houyhnhnms. They are the most rational, best-behaved animals on earth. They never even think anything evil. Yet they have not the least speck of pride—they don't even have a word for it.

But wild, ugly, miserable Yahoos? Why, they're so often full of pride that it disgusts me to think about it.

All I ask, in parting, is that if you're proud yourself, if you think you're something grand, if you think that you're superior to any of the creatures on God's earth, if you think that you have the right to mistreat other animals and boast of it—then please, please, never appear in my sight.

The End

Thanks for reading,
Luke Hayes

I would love to hear from you. Email: LukeHayesAuthor@gmail.com

Visit: http//:Gulliverstravelsforkids.com

Look for more Classics for Kids.

Please be kind to animals.

CPSIA information can be obtained at www.ICGtesting.com
Printed in the USA
BVOW07s2152161114

375370BV00001B/205/P